MOSAIC of *Grace*

A Collection of Short Works

Edited by
Anne Hamilton, Ruth Bonetti & Rosemary New

Armour

Hazel Barker
Linda Barton
Ruth Bonetti
Sonia Couchman
Ingrid Dacker
Diana Davison
Miranda de Jager
Bishop M. Lester Dighton
Terry Gatfield
Jenny Glazebrook

Merridy Glazebrook
Anne Hamilton
Dell Saddler Hamilton
Roseanne Holliday
Michelle Hope
Pamela Julian
Nola Lorraine
Lexia Mackin
Jeanette O'Hagan

Robin Payne
Raelene Purtill
Rebekah Robinson
Judy Rogers
Karen Roper
Linda Shields
Jo Wanmer
YK Willemse
Jenny Woolsey
Justin Yeend

Mosaic of Grace

Anne Hamilton, Ruth Bonetti, Rosemary New (editors)

© Individual contributors 2026

Published by Armour Books
P. O. Box 492, Corinda QLD 4075

Cover & interior design and typeset by Beckon Creative
Images: Sun Sublimation, pikepicture, Design Store | Creative Fabrica

ISBN: 978-1-923533-12-7

A catalogue record for this book is available from the National Library of Australia

Note: Australian spelling and grammar conventions are used throughout this book.

MOSAIC of Grace

A Collection of Short Works

Edited by
Anne Hamilton, Ruth Bonetti & Rosemary New

Contents

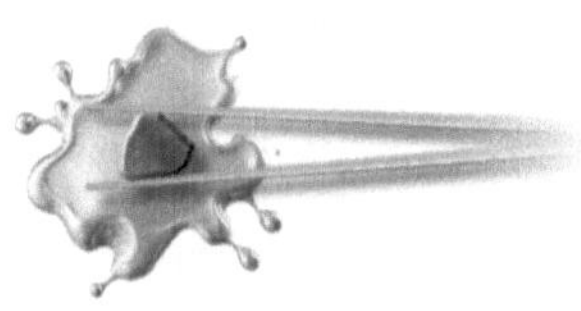

Introduction

ANNE HAMILTON, RUTH BONETTI & ROSEMARY NEW

As each one has received a special gift, employ it in serving one another as good stewards of the multifaceted grace of God.

1 Peter 4:10 NAS

The word, *multifaceted*, that Peter uses to describe grace is the Greek 'poikílos', an adjective resonating with symphonic overtones. It means *varied, many-coloured, variegated, diversified, kaleidoscopic, manifold.*

Thirty contributors to this third anthology have made it truly 'poikílos' in beauty, approach and genre. Works range from poems to essays and from fiction to non-fiction. The theme of this volume is, once again, faith. However, many authors picked up on the pun within the word *mosaic*—a noun for a *tiled and tessellated picture* as well as an adjective for *of Moses*—and styled their gifts to this book accordingly.

We extend our deepest gratitude for those gifts—which enable any profits from these anthologies to go towards releasing brick-kiln slaves in Pakistan.

Please enjoy this collection!

Anne, Ruth + Rosemary

January 2026

NONFICTION

Grace to Speak

JENNY GLAZEBROOK

'We will all write a rap and then perform it for the class.'

Our new year seven music teacher sounded excited, as though he had handed us a beautiful gift to unwrap.

Unrap.

If only I could re-wrap that rap and hand it back to the teacher.

Sitting beside me was my confident, extroverted friend. Across the other side of the room was the group of boys who loved to amuse themselves at my expense—to laugh at the unusual shape of my mouth and nose, and mimic my quiet voice.

I was born with a cleft lip and palate and had been through many surgeries to repair it, but every day I felt as though my lip protruded further and my nose became more crooked. It didn't help that those boys would call out after me with their witty but cruel comments.

I pushed the boys from my mind and did what I loved to do. *Write.* The words to the rap came easily. I loved words. I loved rhyme. But as I sat waiting for my turn to stand up in front of the class and rap along to the beat the music teacher played on the keyboard, my stomach swirled and my heartbeat rose up into my throat, pounding as though it wanted to escape. Like I did.

My friend effortlessly breezed through her perfect rap, and then the teacher looked at me. 'Jenny. Your turn.'

I crept out the front, staring at the floor in an attempt to hide my face. My fingers shook. My voice got stuck in my throat. I missed the first beat, and the teacher gave me a kind look. 'How about we begin again?'

I catapulted through, my voice barely audible, staring down at the words to my rap. My vision blurred, and my hands trembled.

And then it was done. I drew in a shaky breath and charged back to my seat.

'We couldn't hear her,' one of the boys called out.

'Make her do it again,' another called.

The teacher didn't realise they exulted in publicly humiliating me. 'Come back, Jenny, and we'll try again. A bit louder this time,' he said.

I came back. I tried, I truly did, but a heavy blanket of fear and shame muffled my words.

'We still can't hear,' a boy interrupted.

The teacher's hands stilled on the keyboard, then he played the background beat again.

'Still can't hear!' A girl added to the fray.

The torture began again and I blurted out the words, ignoring the beat despite my good sense of rhythm.

The teacher took pity on me and allowed me to go back to my seat where I stared down at the desk, red-faced, ashamed, humiliated.

The teacher approached me later that day. 'Jenny, it was a good rap,' he said, and I saw the apology in his eyes. He'd finally recognised the bullying.

A few weeks later:

'Dad has booked you in to camp for the holidays,' Mum said as I came in the back door after school.

My older sister beamed with joy. She loved Christian camps and would be able to catch up with some special friends she only saw a few times a year.

I didn't share her excitement. I felt sick to the stomach. Camps were filled with … people. People to judge, stare, mock. And even worse, they were Christians. Would they see that I was not worthy to be one of them?

'Self-consciousness is selfishness,' my mother said, and the guilt and shame clawed deeper into my soul. I was shy, anxious, fearful, defensive, and spiteful. But I had no choice. I had to go.

My sister was in her element and tried to help me fit in, but by the second day of camp, I had such severe stomach cramps that I was writhing on my bunk, alone and in agony.

'God,' I cried, 'I've had enough. I can't do this anymore. Please, take my life.' Tears streamed down my cheeks as I raced to the bathroom to be sick.

I staggered up to the manager's house. 'I don't feel well,' I mumbled to the manager's wife through tears. She took pity on me, gave me a hug and allowed me to call my parents to take me home.

'I can't come until after five,' Mum said. Hours away, but I knew how it worked. Dad was working, and Mum couldn't leave the business phone unattended.

I headed back to my bunk but stopped as a beautiful sound filled my ears—music coming from the camp hall—drawing me up the steps instead of down, as though a song was calling me. I crept into the back of the room and sat cross-legged on the floor beside my sister. I always felt safe with her. She was beautiful, confident, popular and oh so spiritual. She called God 'Lord' and prayed eloquently.

She glanced at me and smiled a welcoming but concerned smile, then focused again on the front of the room where a camp leader was singing. It was a song she wrote for a dying friend, rejoicing in the day they would reunite in heaven with Jesus.

Her fingers strummed the strings of her guitar, and the sound was hauntingly beautiful. Her pure voice rose, filling the room with an ethereal warmth. Lightness rose in my spirit as it wrapped around me like a blanket and a knowing, a truth—almost like a voice—spoke into my heart saying, 'I made you this way for a reason. I love you and I can use you just the way you are.'

The presence of Jesus filled me, and for the first time in my life, I felt accepted and loved. This time I didn't beg Him to take my life, I gave it to Him. I offered it up freely, clinging to a hope I had never dared to believe was mine to claim.

I stayed for the full camp. On the way home, I looked out the car window at gum trees and rolling hills—they appeared greener, more vibrant than I'd ever seen them before. The sun was brighter, gentler, warmer, like an embrace, and words flowed through my mind—poems of joy and praise, coming from a source deeper than myself. I knew it was the Lord. My friend.

Being loved made all the difference. I grew in confidence knowing I was not visual pollution in God's eyes, that He accepted my deformity and my weakness, but I was still cautious. Words wanted to bubble out of me, but I held them in and instead wrote poem after poem. I wrote letters to my new Christian friends. I wrote stories, I journalled prayers to God. But my spoken words were still bound by fear.

The day before I was to have major jaw reconstruction surgery, a camp leader phoned me.

'Jenny, I have something I believe the Lord wants me to share with you,' Steve said.

My heart pounded and I waited, wondering what it could be. A rebuke? An encouragement?

'Do you remember when Moses was asked to speak to Pharoah?'

'Yes.'

'Moses asked the Lord to send someone else. He knew he wasn't eloquent. He said he was slow of speech and tongue. He knew his weakness and it held him back.'

I knew exactly how Moses felt. I would try to speak to people and my mind would go blank. I would become so aware of my mouth, my appearance, my deformity, that I could think of nothing else.

'But this is what the Lord said to Moses.' I heard the pages rustling in Steve's Bible. *'Who gave human beings their mouths? Who makes them deaf or mute? Who gives them sight or makes them blind? Is it not I, the Lord? Now go; I will help you speak and will teach you what to say.'*

Why was Steve telling me this? I was about to have major surgery—my jaw would be broken, realigned, and wired back together. I wouldn't be able to eat solid food for six weeks, and the wire binding shut my jaw would trap my tongue, preventing clear speech. Recovery would take more than a year.

Steve's voice came down the phone again, clear but gentle. 'What I felt the Lord wanted me to share with you, is that He can use your weaknesses more than you can ever use your strengths. Just like He did with Moses.'

This truth sank deep into my soul. God made me the way He did for a reason, and He could use me, weaknesses and all. Even Moses feared speaking and yet look how God had used him.

Surgery was traumatic. Painful. Frightening. The recovery was long. I looked different, I felt different, my mind was foggy and I felt trapped within my own body. Even after the wires holding my jaw together were cut, it took months to regain strength. My muscles had wasted away, and as I walked, my teeth clattered together.

But through that time I continued to write, and my love and confidence in God's strength and calling on my life grew.

I shared my testimony at Christian camps and church youth groups, reading directly from my notebook, my voice shaking, but knowing God could use my weakness for His glory. And He did. Many lives were changed.

Eighteen months later:

I stood in front of the microphone in the school hall and looked at the sea of students and teachers. Love for them filled me, along with a sadness that this was my last week of school. Final exams were about to begin.

I glanced at the giggling year seven boys and my heart yearned for them to know that they didn't need to prove themselves, didn't need to hurt others first before they were hurt. I looked at my classmates. Some had confided in me that they were suicidal, or were wrestling with choices about abortion, some were living in broken families… and all I had to offer them was Jesus. But He was more than enough.

It was time. I glanced at my minimal notes, then met the eyes of the students Jesus loved, and I began to speak clearly, with confidence to those who had mocked, bullied, and tormented me.

I shared that God loves each one of us just the way we are and has a purpose for our lives. I shared that we can choose to give our lives to Him, or we can choose to live our own way.

I shared that He can use our weaknesses more than we can use our own strengths. I spoke openly about the shame I had felt, about the pain and emptiness, but how God had filled those places.

And a special friend played the piano accompaniment as I sang in front of the school with my Christian friends who accepted me just the way I was.

My sister was there, but this time I didn't need her to speak for me the way she had done through most of my childhood. No, she was there to cheer me on as I spoke about Jesus, my closest friend. And in my weakness, the Lord was glorified. His strength and the power of His ability to redeem was made known.

To my disappointment, students didn't surrender their lives to Jesus—at least not that day—but God's extraordinary grace was there.

It was there in the once scared, voiceless teenager who stood in front of those who had mocked and bullied her and spoke with absolute confidence of the redeeming love and grace of God.

Like Moses, I had been given grace to speak.

Finding God in a Fairy-tale Castle
JO WANMER

*M*y far-right religious upbringing unsettled me. I drove through lush rain forest inland from Byron Bay. So beautiful and majestic. The road and vegetation didn't disturb me, rather my destination caused my angst.

I was on a weekend retreat with about ten other women celebrating my friend, Margie's, birthday. To be the only Christian in a group was unusual for me, but I was delighted to be there. On the first morning some of the women went to visit a local Fairy-tale Castle. Margie hadn't wanted to go. By nature, I'm inquisitive but my early training caused me to be cautious about going anywhere that could be labelled New Age. We stayed home and were there to welcome a few latecomers. After showing them their rooms we settled on the veranda with drinks and relaxed.

Our accommodation was a rambling house surrounded by trees. Many different birds sang and chattered, their chorus making a delightful background. What a wonderful place to be! As I sat and chatted to women I didn't know, I watched the alcohol flow. That same upbringing left me with no desire to drink.

The other group returned from their adventure full of excitement. They each carried a polaroid photo taken when they had their aura read. We gathered around, intrigued. They all talked at once, reading their summary of what the 'expert' had said about their life. Most of the ladies treated it like a joke, but now everyone else wanted to go to the Castle and have their auras read.

My interest was piqued but I still had reservations. After lunch they gathered to go to the Castle. I wasn't intending to go but, as I looked at the group, I realised they'd all been drinking.

I joined them with an offer. 'I'll drive!' They were quick to agree and piled into my car. The four of them chattered, filled with anticipation at what they'd discover. In the driver's seat I prayed, asking God to cover and protect me. We drove through thick forest, the boughs of the trees holding hands above our heads, reminiscent of a cathedral. So stately. The sun shone through the gaps between leaves, decorating our way with mosaics of light. It wasn't long until we entered a bitumen carpark, dulling the magic.

The Fairy-tale Castle surprised me. The roof had steep pointy hats, styled like a castle, but walls of glass revealed glimpses of large colourful boulders. Now interested, I followed the others, still praying and asking God to protect me from any spirits that weren't from Him.

I stopped, stunned. Such magnificence! Rocks of all shapes and sizes, pulsed with light, colour and beauty. I stood in awe of such splendour and wandered from stone to stone, room to room, marvelling at the colour and patterns. Unbidden my inner spirit had started leaping in praise to my Creator. Inwardly I worshipped with joy.

My companions wandered around, seemingly unmoved. They soon lined up waiting to have their auras taken. I wandered in the opposite direction, absorbing the wonder. My spirit was light. No fear argued with my joy. I walked on, inwardly worshipping my King. My old religious restrictions tried to argue, but the peace in my spirit allowed me to ignore the lies. There was freedom in shaking off that old religious shackle.

Some of the rocks were big enough to sit on. Others were small enough to be crafted into earrings. A few of them were split in half, displaying amazing patterns and colours. I recognised opal and topaz, but not many others. Yet there seemed to be thousands of them.

My companions gathered at the aura station waiting, chattering in anticipation of seeing their picture. A small inkling of an idea stirred, from my curious nature surely. *~Go and have your aura read.~*

Get behind me, Satan! I inwardly rebuked the notion and pushed it aside. To me it seemed similar to having my palm read, or a fortune-teller looking into a crystal ball. It was the work of witchcraft, a counterfeit, designed to lead me away from God.

Walking away from them I wandered towards the back. I realised I was still spontaneously worshipping God in my spirit. There was no sign He was offended, but again delighting to show off the beauty of His creation.

~Go and have your aura read.~ Did that small voice come from God? Once again, I discarded the notion. It couldn't be God, *just couldn't.* I walked toward the exit, seeking a change in atmosphere, some fresh air to clear my thinking.

~Go and have your aura read.~

I stopped. I remembered the Biblical story of Apostle Peter having a vision of unclean animals being lowered in a sheet from heaven. A voice instructed him to eat. He refused, vehemently. The very idea was offensive to his religious training and upbringing… just as this was offensive to me. Peter heard the voice three times before he stopped arguing. Then I understood… The voice I'd heard three times *was* the Lord.

Peter obeyed God which enabled him to go into a Gentile's home and have the opportunity to share about Jesus. Without the vision he would have missed the chance. I didn't understand what God was doing, but chose to push my prejudices aside and trust the God who is bigger than any Fairy-tale Castle. I joined the short line. My spirit rested in peace.

The woman behind the counter was pleasant as she noted my name and took my money. She asked if I'd ever had my aura read before. With the shake of my head, she explained how the process worked, making me feel as though I was the only person she'd met that day. I surveyed the large wooden chair, the back of it higher than my head. Wide wooden boards awaited my arms. Metal plates were attached to electrical wires where my hands would rest. The contraption reminded me of an electric chair used to terminate a criminal's life. I shuddered at the thought and shot another heart prayer to heaven. My inner peace returned so I lowered myself into the chair. It wasn't built for comfort but closer to torture. Placing my hands as shown, legs straight, and head up, I tried to relax, as instructed.

A polaroid camera was carefully adjusted. 'Hold still. There's no need to smile. Just relax.' Several shots were taken, each photo laid in a basket to await development. With a nod the photographer asked me to return in ten to fifteen minutes. They would then read my aura.

I joined the others, no longer separated by my religious entanglements. One by one they returned to the counter to listen to the lady and see their picture. The rest of us watched over their shoulders. All the pictures displayed differing colours of light that emanated from their chest in an elliptical pattern. A haze of colour shaded the background. I stood beside Margie as the woman explained what the colour and lines of light revealed about her. It highlighted the anger she lived in and other struggles. I was stunned by the reading. Although not at all complimentary, it was quite accurate. The reader capsulised everyone's character. She unmasked problems, dropping them as facts, with no promise of help.

Then it was my turn. What would she say?

Lord, help me to remember this is not You. Your words are my real rock.

Margie stood beside me, as curious as I was. The woman pulled out the photo and stared for a minute. She lifted her eyes. 'I've never seen so much forgiveness in any aura.'

Margie muttered, 'That'd be right. She forgives the unforgivable.'

I whispered, 'That would be Jesus.'

The woman continued to comment about the light from my heart, using words like hope and love. But all I could see was the Spirit of God shining from within me, caught on a camera in the devil's playground.

I steered the car back to our retreat through the leafy cathedral, awed by God's beauty and His ways. The conversation for the rest of the day revolved around those pictures, each person studying everyone else's. I was pleased I had a picture to share, so that I could talk about Jesus in me! From the picture of my aura came many opportunities to talk about my Lord.

Next morning, I arose early to walk and pray as I did every day. The enemy's voice was quick to attack me. *You can't pray any more. You broke the law by entering the devil's temple and having your aura read.*

I laughed and corrected him. *No. I nullified the law in my willingness to be obedient to my Saviour.* I asked the Lord for a Scripture to rest my faith on. As I walked the still voice suggested I remember references to stones in the Bible. They flooded my mind. Stones were carefully selected for the temple, for the breastplate the priests wore into God's presence, for rings and ephods.

Then came the words from Isaiah 54:12 TPT, from the chapter the Lord often used to speak to me.

> *I will make your towers of rubies*
> *Your gates of sparkling jewels*
> *And all your walls of precious delightful stones.*

How God basks in the beauty of precious rocks and loves us exalting Him for His handiwork. A Scripture came to mind. *God delights in obedience rather than sacrifice.* I had sacrificed my 'need' to keep myself safe by following my religious thinking. Instead, I chose to walk in obedience under God's protection. All the enemy's accusations fell to the ground.

Have I returned to other New Age sites? No, I haven't.

Not because of religious beliefs which no longer control me.

Now I'm aware God leads me and I follow. He hasn't taken me that way again. That episode was a one-off blessing. What a precious experience… and to think I nearly missed it.

A Divine Opportunity

DELL SADDLER HAMILTON

* I have full permission to tell this story from the woman who was healed. She said: 'Shout it from the rooftops!'

I was at a school of prayer ministry when a woman handed me a slip of paper she'd picked up from the floor. On it was written: *To forgive her would be like forgiving Hitler!*

Deciding discretion was the better part of valour, I chose not to wave it in the air and ask who'd lost it. Instead I hid it under a pile of books.

However it soon became apparent who had written it. Attending the course was young woman in her late twenties who'd been severely disabled in an accident. Jenny was in constant pain. She moved with the aid of a walking frame, had a car modified for her individual needs and, in addition, used a special chair as well as an air mattress on the floor. She couldn't sit or lie for very long and also found it very difficult to stand up.

My husband Jim and I offered her private prayer ministry, and it soon transpired that the *'her'* who'd been compared to Hitler was Jenny's mother.

After hearing her traumatic story, I nevertheless suggested forgiveness as the only way forward. But with venom in her voice, she snarled, 'I will NEVER forgive her!'

I told her I would be too scared of God *not* to forgive and explained why. Only as we forgive others are we forgiven in turn. The conversation then went in another direction, when suddenly, after about twenty minutes she almost spat: 'Oh, alright, I'll forgive her!'

Now, privately I didn't think it sounded much like forgiveness. However we quickly discovered that God will honour even reluctant words. Jim and I prayed, and I told her that, because she *had* forgiven she *was now* forgiven, and she was released from the effects of unforgiveness and bitterness.

Finishing the session, Jim and I returned to the main room to discover everyone else had left. We began to tidy up while Jenny hobbled off to her car using her walking frame. A few minutes later she was back. She rushed in, screaming.

'Look at *me*!' she yelled. 'Look at *me*!'

'Look at *what*?' I asked, not registering.

'I can walk! I can run! And I have no pain... and you didn't even pray for physical healing.'

'Perhaps I didn't have to,' I answered. 'You gave God permission to take the bitterness out of your heart and He took the opportunity to take it out of your bones at the same time!' I wasn't too sure where those words had sprung from. They came out without thought.

'But what on earth am I going to tell Social Security?'

'How about the truth? That God healed you?'

'They'll think I'm crazy.'

Jenny came back the next day, radiant with an almost golden glow around her — without the walking frame, or the mattress or the special chair. The healing turned out to be permanent.

Reflection on Forgiveness:

'Forgive us our sins, as we have forgiven those who sin against us.'

Matthew 6:12 NLT

Forgiveness is not an option. After a very long life I have invariably noticed that those who readily forgive lead lives that are more spiritually, emotionally, mentally and physically healthy than those who find it hard to forgive. I once saw a poster that said: *'To fail to forgive is like drinking poison and expecting the other person to die.'* And that poster was true. Unforgiveness hurts no one nearly as much as the one who harbours it in their heart.

Yet having said that forgiveness is not an option, it is also absolutely impossible. We simply can't do it. But we can be willing to allow God to work through us to achieve it. The woman in this story illustrates this principle. Jenny couldn't do it, but she was willing to speak the words and allow Jesus to empower them within her life.

Prayer:

Father in Heaven: I find it so hard to forgive when another person deliberately dishonours me. I decide to forgive but within a short time those niggling thoughts are back. Father, I want to forgive; please forgive my unforgiveness. Lord, I want to come to You, pure and undefiled. Please wash me clean with the cool, clean waters of Your Holy Spirit washing through every cell in my body—through my heart, spirit, mind and soul until I am squeaky clean and spotless, free of all defilement.

I ask this in the name of my Lord and Saviour, Jesus Christ. Amen.

I Knew a Lad

BISHOP M. LESTER DIGHTON

He had a reputation for being 'accident-prone'. His body had scars from burns, deep wounds, grazing, and bruising. His right elbow had been dislocated. He was no stranger to pain, not just from what happened to him, but from chronic pain in his joints. There was no doubt that he belonged to that family, as he looked just like his siblings. However, that is where the similarities ended; he just wasn't the same, and always felt like an outsider. He enjoyed talks on poetry and philosophy with his father, and even ventured into philosophy himself. His father constantly urged him to 'Think about it', and this became a bit of a motto for him.

At eleven, he started drinking alcohol, and he found that it eased the pain. By thirteen, he was an alcoholic, who only wanted to write himself off at every occasion. It was easier then.

He contracted osteomyelitis, which saw him in hospital for months. Radical surgery, almost an amputation, and a trial drug.

He also saw things at times that the others didn't, and they didn't like him talking about the way things were going to happen. They used to treat him badly over this. He did all sorts of things just to fit in.

Another vision, and this time, he drowned; tangled in weeds. He went out to get a giant pearl to give to someone he loved, and he was given that pearl but, while trying to surface, the weeds dragged him down and he drowned. A pretty serious dream for one so young, and, to make matters worse, that dream came often. The very next day, he was sent into a weeded creek to retrieve a canoe left there, but he froze. He remembered drowning in the weeds in that dream. He was given a beating and left crying on the bank.

They did not understand—he didn't understand, so how could they?

That led to frequent beatings, and they even made a game of hunting him for sport, and being caught meant another beating. The lad learned to become almost invisible amongst the grass and bush. His reflexes quickened as he evaded random attacks.

Around the age of fifteen, matters took several turns. First, he secured an apprenticeship. Next, while trying to evade a thrashing, he smashed his left knee on some rocks. After this, he was riding his pushbike along the highway to go to an event. Even though he was off the road, the vehicle struck him from behind. He bounced off the windscreen and was thrown into the bush. He spent overnight in hospital, then was sent home, apparently ok. That Christmas, he was thrown into a rock wall; face first. He got himself off the rocks, where he was taken to hospital. No doctor on duty. They stitched him up without anaesthetic (no real place to put the needle); all the while he spat out blood and bits of teeth. He damaged his neck in that incident. He had three days off work.

The lad suffered from PTSD from that time on, and had to hide it whenever possible, but sometimes he just couldn't. When he saw someone hurt, he would collapse. Studying medicine didn't work; he was useless with someone seriously injured.

Every piece of security was becoming broken and shattered for him.

He threw himself into his work more and more, and the dreams and visions stopped. What a relief!

He ran away from home after this. Not everything went to plan, and he ended up living on the streets. His alcoholism grew worse, and he also added drugs to the equation.

He entered into areas of study in the occult. He quickly advanced, where he was led to other fields of study. However, the more he studied, the more an itch he couldn't scratch went on inside. The alcohol and drugs were not helping that itch either. Each new study eased it for a while, but nothing stopped that itch. Every time he thought he was managing to rearrange the pieces of pottery into a new vessel that was worth something, it would become broken again.

As he did not know how to relate to others properly, he became something of a shy lad, but his father severely rebuked him—*understatement*—over that for 'conning' people.

There were a couple of things that happened during this era that did not fit the normal way of things. One was that someone gave him a Bible Passage and it spoke about Two Witnesses. These had the power to shut up heaven, and cause the rain to stop. This was a subject that the lad could understand, as he was learning in the occult how to control the weather using spirits and forces!

Secondly, he came to realise he was only acting on other's ideas of what to do. He contemplated what he was doing, and decided that, in one week's time, he would give up alcohol, cigarettes, and drugs. Well, the next day, he stopped alcohol, drugs, cigarettes, coffee, and meat. All on the one day. He just woke up that morning and didn't touch them.

He quit his job and went hitch-hiking around Australia. It was this time spent walking the highways where he had time to reflect on how it was working out — or not. He contemplated Truth, but *what was it?*

He came to the conclusion that Truth must exist, but how do you go about finding it? In desperation, he cried out to the air around him: 'Truth, if you are out there—show yourself! If you are real, then let me see you!'

One thing he soon learned after that is that you have to be very careful about what you ask for—you may just get it!

He was picked up just north of Ingham, and taken to Cairns. He was asked to stay with the chap and his friends, and so he did, and was invited to go to their church. It was on the second visit that the Pastor called for anyone who needed to come to God to come up!

Up the lad went, and the Pastor went to the lad, and prayed over him. The lad fell down on his knees in fear and trembling—not knowing what was happening. The voice rumbled inside his head: 'Come here, I want to talk with you.'

When you go seeking God, He will find you!

Things changed after that, not all at the same time. The Pastor asked him what now, and the lad replied that he needed to go bush and think on this. He went out to central Queensland, and started a new life there on the sheep and cattle properties.

Around this time, he met a gentleman who took him under his wing, and taught him so much of Christianity, including a more contemplative way. The lad took another look at his occult teachings, and saw how different they were from God's ways.

The pieces were coming together, but others would still end up very broken. You see, the lad was changing, not just in his manners, but in how he approached and did things. His partner did not understand the changes in him, but he continued on, for something was starting to scratch that itch inside. This created problems within the relationship — she wanted the man he used to be.

He fought much of Christianity with tooth and nail. There had to be faults in this system, just as there was in all the others—he just had to find them. The harder he tried to find faults, the less he found he could.

He now wanted to get it right, but he did not always act in God's Love automatically. No. The Letter of the Law was important. His partner tried to follow, but it was too alien for her, and so it became something of a toxic relationship. What was supposed to be a wonderful life was a jumble of pieces and shards, and yet God's Grace was still working around him. He heard a person mention the Pearl of Great Price in the Bible, and what it meant. That fateful dream came again that night, but he didn't drown this time. That dream never came again.

He went to work in Sydney as he studied, and this proved to be a wonderful grounding, but also a time of long hours, and full schedules. He needed a break, and so he went back to the bush, where he could commune with God in His Creation. God still had much to show him in Creation.

He realised that he needed to hand it over to God, and so he did. Years of trying to do it for God, instead of *with* God. It just didn't work that way.

Eventually, he was told, 'Go to the city,' and so he did. He found some work and started to go to church. This wasn't an option out west. The workloads and distances were distinct barriers to that. He met up with another friend from years earlier, who introduced him to the Bishop where he went to church. They were introduced, and became friends. This led to the lad being asked to become a Deacon, as the Bishop liked the lad's knowledge of Scripture. After time in prayers, he became ordained as a Deacon, then Priest, and then went on to become a Bishop himself.

All of this after much prayer and service in the church. However, that is not the end of the story for the lad, as he asked for autocephalic status, so that he could again go back to the bush to serve those who did not have churches. This was granted, and this began the next phase of the lad's journey.

Despite everything the lad endured, including ongoing injuries and incidents, which never really stopped over the years; he continued on with hope always in his heart. Fractured vertebrae and broken bones; bumps, scrapes, and with emotional bangs and crashes. The physical pain never stopped for him, only varied in degree, daily.

God kept on teaching him the Holy Word of God, and what it means to us. This was no easy task, and it was aided by dreams and visions. This time they were different. They weren't just about local people and events, but often on a much larger scale. Even those that were more personal had a greater context to them. Things had certainly changed. The pieces were coming together again, but the overall picture was still not clear. For starters, the lad still felt lonely. He spent time looking at himself, and wondered if he *needed* to be married, or just *wanted* to be married. He came to the conclusion that he wanted to be married, and build good memories together with someone.

Now this is a whole new ballgame with some scary things to be addressed here. Where do you find a good Christian woman? Every time he thought he might have found someone, things went pear-shaped. His choices were clearly not the best choices. He eventually decided that, if God had someone for him, then God would have to bring her to him.

Long story short, they ended up married. A lovely woman, who was also a keen adherent to Christianity, and together they have finally put their individual broken pieces together to make a wonderful picture for all to see. I like to see this picture in action, for it is a blessing to see a fulfilment like this for them. A new picture made from all the broken shards and pieces, telling a completely new story.

I suppose that you are wondering how I know this lad so well, and even how I stayed in touch with him for so long?

Well, that lad is me!

Y. K. WILLEMSE

7:24 am. Chinchilla Hospital car park.

'Are you going to be all right buckled in?' Michael asked.

'I can't sit like that,' Yvette told him. 'I'll sort it out. Don't you worry about it. Just drive.'

They climbed into the Hyundai Tucson. It was hot already. The aircon was still broken. Yvette arranged towels on the floor and snacks on the front passenger seat. She knelt on the floor facing her Mars bars on the seat.

She had been storing these up. With her firstborn Holly, she'd barely eaten any chocolate during pregnancy. In labour, she had eaten an entire lunchbox of chocolates she'd brought with her to hospital.

Hospital.

Chinchilla Hospital didn't do births. Yvette and Michael had known this and planned the upcoming birth in Dalby like everyone else. The nurse on the floor today had insisted they had time to get to Dalby, an hour away. They had only come in for an appointment, brought forward two hours because of more early labour.

We're lucky, Yvette thought. Two weeks of early labour had worried Yvette. Floods had cut Chinchilla off from Dalby. Would it be a wild helicopter ride to Toowoomba? At church they had sung *Mary, Did You Know?* with its haunting question about giving birth in a stable. But God had taken care of her even when people had failed.

And the floodwater around Dalby had subsided recently.

He'll take care of us.

They pulled away from the hospital. Yvette held onto the passenger seat.

7:31. Gosden's Machinery. The Warrego Highway. 71 kms to go.

Every small country town in Queensland seemed to have a graveyard of old, rusty cars and tractors outside of it. Yvette had often noticed this since immigrating from New Zealand with Michael in 2019.

'What's the make of your car?' Linda the midwife had said before they even got to the Hyundai in the hospital car park. 'I need to know what I'm looking for.'

Yvette's midwife could follow her to Dalby Hospital. That, at least, was allowed. Linda had been in a state of concern for the last two weeks with all Yvette's early labour episodes.

'I had a dream the other night I came to your house and only just got there as the head came out,' Linda had told her.

Breathe, two, three, four, five. Hold, two, three, four, five. Out, two, three, four, five, six, seven. Were they coming closer together now? Yvette had a mild sinking feeling as Gosden's Machinery disappeared in the rear windscreen.

'You're doing great,' Michael said.

7:34. Brigalow township. The Warrego Highway. 64 kms to go.

The dance hall was still draped with cheerful Christmas decorations. Yvette tried to think about the dance she and Michael had enjoyed there. Labour was relentless. And messy. Disgusting. Her heat pack from the hospital had stopped working. Though she bashed the other two into submission, neither wanted to work.

Don't think about it, she told herself, cleaning up down there yet again.

There wasn't enough time to properly chew on a Mars bar between contractions, which meant labour was officially not fun anymore. Yvette's meditation music blared through the car speakers. Flowing water, twittering birds. Her groans competed with it.

Stay positive. Beatrix needs you, she told herself.

They had chosen Beatrix as their baby's name. A nod to Yvette's Dutch blood and their faith, it had been popular among early Christian pilgrims, meaning *blessed traveller*.

'Soon we'll meet Beebee.' Michael drove them from Brigalow. 'One town down.'

'God, keep us safe today. Protect us and our baby,' Yvette whispered.

7:45. Warra township. 47 kms to go.

There were no turns between Chinchilla and Dalby. Just 80 kms of Warrego Highway. Yvette, Michael, and their eighteen-month-old firstborn Holly had travelled it many times. Today it felt extra long.

The second heat pack had started working just out of Brigalow, but its benefits quickly faded. It felt like an anvil had just wedged itself in the small of Yvette's back. Each contraction was a great wave. She tried to imagine kayaking (a favourite pastime) and riding the waves, using them to bring her close to her destination.

The new gas station in Warra was ahead.

'Michael, can we stop? See if they've got a shower or something?'

The car floor around her knees was revolting, and there was nothing for the pain relief. No aircon either. Maybe they would have aircon? A shower out back?

'We have to keep going,' Michael said.

The gas station flashed past.

Ugh, seriously? Breathe, two, three, four, five. Hold, two, three, four, five. Release, two, three, four, five, six, seven. She had to repeat this three times for each contraction, and her small groans had become a full, loud vocalisation.

Nobody would think I know anything about singing right now, she thought. What was that *Messiah* aria she'd been listening to at home while doing pregnancy exercises?

Come unto Him all ye that labour. She was certainly labouring now.

She steeled herself as Warra disappeared too.

'Just Macalister to go,' Michael said.

After Macalister, Dalby. Still, it felt like the nurse that had sent them on hadn't thought this through.

Yvette couldn't trust the medical staff at present. All the stupid COVID rules! If you were a close contact, isolate for a week or however long it was. She couldn't be separated from her husband and eighteen-month-old daughter at this time. And the mask mandates in the hospital! Yvette always felt like she was suffocating. At least she could breathe here.

I have everything I need in this car. Michael will help me if I ask him. And God is with us. Beatrix, God is with us. We'll be okay.

Breathe, two, three, four, five…

7:55. Macalister. 27 kms to go.

Macalister consisted of some massive silos and flocks of galahs exploding in the morning sky. The pain was enormous. It wanted to rip her apart.

It won't, Yvette told herself. *Focus.*

So far on her short journey of motherhood, she had had very few moments of clarity. But this was one of them. She knew without a doubt she would do anything for this child. And she was. She was doing whatever it took.

Breathe, one, two, three, four… it was too much. She was being squeezed like a tube of toothpaste on its last gasp, and she couldn't breathe anymore. The weight in her back was inexorable. Organs and bones were being ground to powder.

Yvette wailed in pain before getting a grip.

Pace yourself, Yvette. We've still got the last stint at the hospital to go.

Instead of breathing through contractions, she switched to blowing. She annihilated imaginary birthday candles. *Puff. Puff. Puff.* The pain was slightly easier to bear.

Yvette forced herself to look at galahs and cockatoos flapping in the sky again. *Immigration!* That had been a wild ride. Yet, this was what she had always wanted—a blue sky, cockatoos screeching against it. Sunshine and light and space. Everything Queensland had given her. God had brought them to a beautiful place. The thought overwhelmed her with peace. He had always travelled with them. He was carrying her and Beatrix safely in His hand.

God, take care of us now.

The next contraction hit like a tidal wave, and she began blowing out imaginary candles again.

An internal, silent explosion. As Macalister flashed by, she dropped her hand from the passenger seat momentarily. An immense weight slid down to rest between her upper thighs. The feeling of fullness in her pelvic floor was unmistakable.

Yvette could touch Beatrix's scalp.

'Michael, I'm crowning. We have to stop! I'm crowning!' she hollered.

The windows were open because the aircon wasn't working. Above the howl of the highway, Michael called back: 'Okay. You think you're crowning? Okay. I'll just find a safe place to stop.'

He was strangely calm, but also incredulous.

'*You think you're crowning…*' I KNOW *I'm crowning*, Yvette thought.

The next contraction rolled on. If she kept blowing out candles, the baby would be there in a heartbeat, born on top of all the mess she had created in the front passenger seat floor space.

Beatrix deserves better. God, help me hold on.

Yvette switched back to breathing through contractions, even though the pain tripled.

They weren't making it to Dalby Hospital. She would give birth outside with the cockatoos and galahs. That was the best she could do.

8:01. Ranges Gully. Approximately 15 kms to go.

It felt like forever before Michael stopped. He rejected a short resting bay in favour of a longer one, close to the tiny road bridge labelled Ranges Gully. The minute the car pulled to a stop, Yvette struggled to her feet, holding onto her sagging baby bump. Wrestling the car door open, she stepped out onto the asphalt. The road was quiet. Third of January. Not a lot of traffic after New Year's.

So many things could go wrong. So many things *wouldn't* go wrong. Yvette couldn't think that way.

God, help us.

He was there—an answering warm, all-encompassing Presence, holding her.

'Help me get my shorts down properly, Michael,' she urged. 'Help me, help me.'

Michael raced around the side of the car. 'I'm helping you,' he said, assisting.

'We need to call Linda right now.' Yvette talked fast. She could feel another contraction coming. This would be it. No more waiting.

'She's right there!'

Michael pointed. Linda the midwife had pulled over her work car in the resting bay behind them.

'Are you all right?' she yelled, grabbing her midwifery bag. 'I'm coming.'

Thank God. The next contraction hit. Yvette's hands dropped instinctively down. *Puff. Puff. Puff.* It was like blowing an enormous bubble from her pelvis. The pain lessened as she allowed Beatrix's head to slide out. As she stood there, she pointed her knees towards each other to avoid tearing. Linda was there. Yvette moved her arms to give her space. She could feel Linda's hands, searching, checking, waiting.

'Do you think we should call an ambulance?' Michael said in the background. 'She's in a lot of pain.'

'It's okay, I've got the head right here,' Linda said.

'Whoa.' Michael grabbed Yvette's shoulder for a moment. 'Did you hear that? The head's out! That's great!'

Faint amusement passed across Yvette's face.

The next contraction followed rapidly.

Nearly there. Puff. Puff.

'I'm just going to wait here like this for the shou–'

A weight glided down swiftly. Feet left Yvette's body with a butterfly flutter. Linda's reaction was instant.

'My baby, did you get her, my baby—'

'There's your baby.' Linda flipped Beatrix over deftly and laid her on Yvette's chest. Yvette wrapped arms around her—this warm, wet, breathing, heart-pounding tiny little lump.

'You did it!' Michael cheered. 'You did it, that's amazing, it's over!'

'Is she breathing, is she all right?'

Yvette pulled Beatrix off her for a second. Eyes screwed tight against the brilliant 30° sunshine, Beatrix mewled. Yvette pulled her back in.

'Right, Dad, a blanket, wrap that baby,' Linda told Michael as she dialled a number on her phone.

Michael covered Beatrix and took a quick photo of mother and daughter together.

8:06 Warrego Highway

Yvette was back in the car with Beatrix on her chest, attached by the umbilical cord. Linda drove, and Michael followed behind in her car as they headed to Dalby Hospital.

Thank You, God, Yvette managed to think before the shaking set in.

January 3rd was her walking through the Red Sea moment. She didn't choose it. It wasn't ideal. Hospital staff had messed up. There was no pain relief. She was scared. But she could trust the God that led her and Beatrix safely through.

Yvette gazed down at her dark-haired, snuffling daughter wrapped in a blanket against her as the car rolled on to its final destination.

Beatrix, *blessed traveller.* Try calling that a coincidence.

A Special Sign

DIANA DAVISON

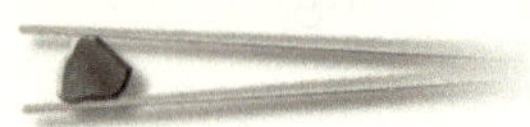

It was seventeen days shy of what would have been my mother's eighty-eighth birthday. The morning I awoke downhearted. It had been two months since her burial, and I couldn't understand why I had received no spark from her, subtle or otherwise. I knew God was listening to my thoughts and prayers, but why wasn't she?

When my father passed away a few years earlier, I had a few visions—significant dreams with him in them. It allowed me to feel connected to him, albeit his city is now celestial and mine civic. But after my mother died—nothing. No fleeting dream. No hovering butterfly. Not even a boo. And so, I decided to call my sister on the other side of the globe. The different time zones meant it was well after midnight at her location and definitely bedtime. But she was awake and yet to lean into her pillow and succumb to much-needed shut-eye.

This phone talk was the first occasion we had spoken to each other since returning from the memorial ceremonies and services in Sarawak back in June. So I cut straight to the point to ask her if she had any kind of message from our departed mother following the funeral. My sister mentioned she had had a dream but not a great deal else. I share; I've had none. I also stupidly confessed to questioning whether our mum loved me given the silence. The grievous grip of grief has many phases. I listen to consoling words—our mother, of course, loved all her children—soothing me aside from silly speculations. We reminded each other of how hard it got for mum towards the final stage. And though she could not speak or see—she sensed we were present, cradling her hand. Conversation soon shifted to mum's gemstones, gold rings and pearl necklaces. The valuables she amassed and treasured the most and derived satisfaction from in her life. Our dad ensured her happiness to the best of his ability. This was her inheritance gift to her offspring and grandchildren after her end.

To me, the absence of any cryptic clues from my mother rendered my emptiness emptier. For a considerable while when she was alive, the mind baggage weighed over the limit. Incurable cancer that riddled *her* body turned *my* existence unpredictable. Days, months, years—how long? The arranging of regular trips abroad to visit her every several weeks. All the affecting and laborious sorting of mum's hoard of belongings. Calculating each contact at divided moments—in between meals and sleep routines. Countless communications and conversations with doctors and staff. The management of her care home bills and provisions. Each day, these responsibilities all sat forefront in my head. Constant tenants that left no scope to consider anything in the short or lengthy term. A list of squatters squeezing personal tasks and time into a small solitary box. Its lid lifted at random bursts, then closed for extended periods, waiting on momentum to pick up where projects, plans and pleasure stalled in a perpetual holding pattern. This heaviness had been a lot of seasons in the crafting and had a firm foothold. But now, there is a peculiarity to the calm. The load lightened, but the reality of lightness is sadness.

After nearly an hour, we concluded the chat—her bed beckoned, and I had household duties to press on with. The clock once again ticked to a steadier beat. But the soft whip still cracked to carry on with chores. And so, I headed down to the cleaning area to feed the washing machine a clothes mountain. But I decided beforehand to go outside to check the mailbox. As I unlocked the glass screen doors, something caught my eye. A strangeness on the core of a tree in the front courtyard—curious and crooked. This motionless cluster remained visible on the trunk directly facing the laundry room. The image captured my interest instantly. Taking a slow approach, I crouched down to further inspect the showy site. The display was of dazzling design. There on the speckled brown bark clung a dozen amazing-looking critters. So beautiful in their mosaic metal-like armour.

I had never actually seen or experienced these vivid jewel beetles before—a natter with my hairdresser later and Google search helped me figure them out. And here they were in my garden, opposite the space where I spend way too much of my life. If ever my family can't find me, they simply have to step into my laundry lackey world. Any parent knows that washing articles of clothing is a never-ending workload. Anyway, I thought it crazy and coincidental of how the subject of my mum cherishing her jewellery and how I spent the initial hours of the morning discussing the very thing with my sibling overseas. These beings were right there, lingering in plain view. It was impossible for me not to notice them.

And just like that—I receive an indicator. The significance of this unexpected and unannounced presence on a woody plant is surreal. These metallic blue-green and red jewel bugs made the delivery. Almost akin to the twelve apostles carrying upon their backs my mother's adornments and reassurance. For me, it is symbolic of transformation and rebirth, of individual growth, change and new beginnings. Silently they existed there to let me know I am not overlooked and one can discover beauty in the unknown. A portion of prized gems and gold she once wore remains with me—a tangible reminder of her. Dreams might be forgotten. Memories will fade. But signs are all around in the wonders of the natural environment and creation. And although I shall miss my mother daily, I merely need to pay attention, accept and acknowledge the nature of things.

On tree trunk outside laundry room — twelve jewel bugs pose
(12 August 2025)

Impossible

INGRID DACKER

'Leigh is due for parole next year. I hope she has been doing some courses and preparing herself for life on the outside.' Jasmine's voice was kind as she spoke. 'She has been in prison for such a long time now. Life will be hard for her, if she hasn't.'

I moved to the lounge and put my phone on speaker so I could give my friend my full attention.

She continued in the same vein for half a minute before I interjected. 'Jasmine, do you know how remarkable that is for you to be saying that?"

'What do you mean?'

'Listen to yourself! Do you see what an amazing work God has done in you?'

Jasmine hadn't given it a thought. It had just flowed out of her.

What was so remarkable about this conversation?

Many years before, with the help of two male accomplices, Leigh had taken Jasmine's sister's life and had left her young nephew an orphan. It had shattered Jasmine. It was as if everything stable and precious was blown into a thousand scattered, splintered pieces. Employment, finances, family and friendships—all upended, broken and bleeding. There was intense scrutiny from the media all throughout three very long, drawn-out court cases and beyond. Jasmine sat through all of it as every minute detail of the morbid, heinous crime was dissected, hearing things that nobody should ever be subjected to, until finally a verdict was reached.

Leigh had been convicted of the murder of Jasmine's sister and brother-in-law.

How do you even begin to process that? How do you keep going? 'Trauma' doesn't come close to describing it.

A woman! How could a woman do such a thing? At first, the bitter thoughts would rise like gall in Jasmine's throat and she would turn again and again to Yeshua for help. She clung to Him. He was her life even when she felt totally numb on the inside. It took some time but slowly, painfully she began the work of forgiving this woman…

Healing came bit by bit, not just from this devastating blow but also from childhood trauma and painful memories that surfaced as a result.

She would only just start to feel like she was gaining some sense of equilibrium when there would be another phone call, another mention of the horrible past, another blow, another round of triggering. There were times it felt like the pain and grief would never end.

But there finally came a day when Jasmine felt that the work of forgiveness was finally done. She felt free, with a lightness in her heart and thoughts. Life was beginning to come together in some sort of normality when Yeshua asked her a very personal, probing question: *Would she be willing to share eternity with Leigh?*

It was almost as if He was asking for Jasmine's permission to bring this woman, this murderer to Himself. *Really?* Confronting in the extreme, this felt completely impossible. In fact it was impossible… absolutely… except for one thing—or rather one Person: Yeshua Himself. The one who said, *'Father, forgive them, they don't know what they're doing.'*

I wept with my friend as she wrestled with herself and with God until she came to a place where she was willing for Yeshua to do the work in her. It was hard—so very hard—and I am so proud of her.

There are people in Jasmine's circle of friends who would have no idea of what she has gone through. It is not something to be casually mentioned around the dinner table. Yet God has seen every tear, every stab of pain. He has wept with her, rejoiced at each baby step forward. He has seen her determination to hold on to His goodness when it was as if the earth had crumbled from beneath her feet and she felt stranded and alone. He sees… He knows…every tear is stored in a bottle with her name on it.

That is why what flowed from Jasmine's heart that day—care for a woman who had done so much harm, who had been languishing in prison for such a long time, care that she be ok in the outside world—was so very remarkable.

Jasmine may not see herself as one of the heroes of faith… but I do and I believe God does too.

(NAMES HAVE BEEN CHANGED)

The Chair

A True Story

NOLA LORRAINE

(D)octor Dan rolls me down the hallway and through the lounge room of his apartment. He's updated the decor since I was here last. Black and white furnishings, abstract prints on the walls and... 'Oww!' He bumps me out the door and onto his third-floor balcony. I wonder why he...

'Hey, watch where you're putting your hands!'

He hefts me up at an awkward angle and hauls me down the stairs.

'Oww!' One of my legs thwacks against a railing. 'Be careful!' Another thwack.

In the foyer, we pass a chair in plastic wrap, just like me when I first arrived off the factory floor. 'Hello there. Are you... Oww!'

Dan whacks my backrest on the doorpost as he manoeuvres me through the gravel carpark and deposits me on the footpath. I spin round, but he's already heading back inside.

'No use lookin' back, kid,' a deep voice resonates beside me. 'You're dead to 'im now.'

I swivel left and face a wooden bookcase with a broken shelf.

'Nev's the name,' he says. 'Apartment 2B.'

'What are we doing out here?' I ask.

'Kerbside collection. Brisbane City Council.'

If I could frown, I'd be doing it now. 'I don't know what that is.'

'You will soon enough. The garbage truck's already picked up the stuff in Vernon Street. Our turn can't be far off.'

'Garbage truck?'

'Off to the tip. The dump. Landfill. Unless some scavenger picks us up first.'

Scavenger? That sounds as bad as landfill.

'Here comes a likely suspect now,' Nev says.

There's a girl walking down the opposite side of the street with two dogs—one white and one gold. She stops for a moment and looks in our direction, then tugs the fluffballs towards us. The dogs give me a good sniff, while the girl looks me up and down. There are strands of grey sprinkled through her chestnut hair and crinkly lines around her eyes.

'Look lively,' Nev says. 'I think this sheila might be interested in you.'

But she looks strained to me, like she's carrying a weight heavier than the dogs. She tips me over and looks underneath, then sets me upright and sits on my extra-wide seat. She caresses my armrests—ooh, that feels nice—then grabs the lever underneath and pumps me up and down. She stands up and rubs her fingers along my back, then ... walks away. Just like that. I let out a puff of compressed air.

'Never mind,' Nev says.

The sky's getting bluer. The sun's getting higher. My butt's getting warmer.

A small white car heads our way and parks right in front of us. It's the girl without dogs. My wheels do a little 'Whee!'

'Looks like she's taking you, after all,' Nev says.

She lifts me with a grunt. I know I'm no lightweight, but this is embarrassing. She tries to shove me through the back door, but nearly knocks a leg off. She drops me back on the ground and moves the front seat forward as far as it will go. Tries to get me in again. *Eek!* Not that way. Even I can see you can't put a round peg in a Nissan-shaped hole. She tries this way and that for ages, but I'm still not in. She plonks me down and grimaces as she does a couple of back stretches. I hope I haven't aggravated anything. She looks defeated.

'Don't give up,' I yell, but she doesn't understand chair-speak.

She braces herself and rams me in at a different angle. I'm going to get kinks in my armrests at this rate, but... we're in... even if my derrière is unceremoniously pressed against the window. 'Bye, Nev.' He tips his broken shelf in a wave.

I don't have time to get a cramp in my wheels because the car pulls into a driveway and she drags me out and carries me up a big flight of stairs at the front of a weatherboard house. A grey-haired woman greets us at the door.

'Can you believe someone was going to throw this out?' the girl says as she wheels me into the house. 'The upholstery's a little worn, but otherwise it's perfect. It's even my colour.'

Perfect? Her colour? I'm not sure what you'd call me. Some shade of red? Dusky pink? Salmon surprise?'

'I'm going to call it Rose.'

Rose? My nuts and bolts do a little jig. I'm a perfect rose.

She wheels me into an office and positions me under a tiny desk. It has a map of the solar system on it. Pluto's still a planet and all the distances are marked in miles.

I eavesdrop when she's on the phone that night, talking to someone called Hunsy or Honey Bunny or something. 'Mum and I were there when they changed the dressing on Dad's wound today. He was nearly climbing the walls in pain and I think the meds are affecting his head.'

The Hunsy person says something I can't hear.

'Oh, I almost forgot. You know how my back's been killing me without an ergonomic chair? I found one that had been tossed out for the kerbside cleanup, but you wouldn't believe the trouble I had getting it in the car. I was about to give up, when I felt like God said, "Do you want the chair or don't you?"' She laughs. A lovely tinkly laugh that warms my springs.

'Then an idea popped into my mind about something different I could try and it worked. It had to be God. I'd never even been down that street before. A real answer to prayer.'

I've never been an answer to prayer before.

We fall into a routine. She sits on me every morning and works on her laptop. Then she and the Mum lady go to visit Dad at the hospital. They come home each day, exhausted and sad.

She plays a song over and over on her phone. Something about a *Waymaker*. She closes her eyes and moves her arms as if she's conducting an orchestra. Sometimes she raises a hand to the ceiling as if she's pushing away the dark or reaching for the light. I hum the tune when she's not there, wondering who this Waymaker is.

She rings the Hunsy person again. 'They said we wouldn't be able to get Mum an aged-care assessment for seven weeks, but we got a cancellation for tomorrow.' She seems pleased about this, though she misses the Hunsy person.

Another phone call, another night. 'They found a nursing home with rooms for Mum and Dad right next to each other. Mum wants to make one a double bedroom and the other a sitting room. Only God could have sorted that out so quickly.'

The next day, the girl and Mum go out the door with suitcases and boxes and bags and dogs. I hear the car backing out of the garage. Then it's quiet. Too quiet. All that day and all that night. And the next. And the next. The office window is closed. The curtains are drawn. I swivel towards the door, but there's no one to push me out. My seat sags. I'm alone.

I try to count off the days on the wall calendar above the desk, but it's hard to keep track. *Twelve days? Fourteen? More?*

And then one day... the garage door creaks open. She's back, but by herself this time. She works day and night. Sorting through things. Packing boxes. Taking things down to the bin.

She finds an old suitcase of handmade baby clothes under a bed. She lingers over each little dress and crocheted jacket, fingering stitches made with love. She spreads them out on the bed and takes photos of each one. A faraway look crosses her face, but then she's back to work again. Sorting, packing, binning.

A pretty woman with long dark hair comes to discuss the sale of the house. The girl talks to Hunsy on her phone. 'Carolyn thinks we can get a good price if we do some renovations. She's going to organise it all.'

Then one morning, she comes into the office and takes a photo of the room. I smile in case it's for the *Officeworks* catalogue. She picks up a marker pen, writes something on a big piece of paper and sticks it to my backrest. I can see the letters through the paper, but I don't know what they mean. TOOWOOMBA.

I watch her through the door as she takes photos of all the rooms and adds notes to an object here, a pile there. She carts a lot of things downstairs. Up and down, up and down, up... and then she lingers, a shadow on her face.

'Thank you, God, for our happy home.' Her voice breaks. I want to wipe the tears from her eyes, but she heads out the door and doesn't come back.

There's nothing to peel away the darkness until the early morning light filters through the flimsy curtains in my room. An hour passes, maybe two, and then there's a commotion outside. A stocky woman with a blonde ponytail struts in and barks instructions to her helpers. 'That's for recycle, that's for the dump, that goes in the truck.''

Back and forth they go, room by room, in and out, up and down. Working like little beavers all day. One of the men eventually lugs me downstairs and shoves me in a minivan.

Am I marked 'recycle' or 'dump'? We bump along, no room to swivel, furniture and bric-a-brac crammed into every nook and cranny. A night in another garage, then we're rattling along. I can hear cars zooming past. It takes forever and I'm starting to feel sick. Then we're at an angle, as if the van's climbing up... up... up. *Is the dump on top of a mountain?*

We level out just as I think I'm going to throw up. We drive for ten minutes, fifteen, then stop. The van door opens and the blonde lady puts me on a paved driveway.

'Brilliant,' says a familiar voice. 'You brought the chair.'

The girl, *my* girl, is waiting. She waves goodbye to the van lady and wheels me into a brick house, down the hallway and into another office. There's an L-shaped desk and a green and black chair is already parked in front of a computer facing one wall. She slides me under the other stretch of desk that faces a window. I can see out onto a patio and across a yard with a high wooden fence. The girl sits down, adjusts my height, and declares, 'Perfect.' The dogs give me a welcome sniff. The Hunsy person comes in for a look.

'Isn't it great?' she says. 'Now that I've got two chairs, I won't have to keep adjusting the height when I move from computer work to desk work. It's even my colour.' She runs her hand across my back. 'I know it's only a small thing in the grand scheme. But when I was down there looking after Mum, trying to get my work done while everything else was going south, it was as if God was saying, "I've got you. I've even picked out this chair so you don't hurt your back. I've got this."'

A warm tingle spreads across my sumptuous seat. Hunsy and the girl head out to the kitchen. I do a full 360° in my new room. The bookcase, the window, and an abstract watercolour on the wall above her desk that looks like someone hanging from a cross. I feel I know Him, as if I've heard of Him before. A soothing presence, even with the thorns that crown His head.

I sink my wheels into the carpet and look out across the lawn. Marked for landfill...

...no more.

Bestie from Boigu Island

RUTH BONETTI

*W*e became besties within an hour of meeting in Canberra, while protest marching to Parliament House on 12 February 2022. An indigenous lady with John 3:16 emblazoned across her T-shirt asked, 'Would you film me, please? I need to preach here.'

Laurel Pabai from the Torres Strait lifted her megaphone and called, 'We are one people of this nation, regardless of the colour of our skin. We need to return to the Creator to heal our land.'

Many affirmed her with pats on her shoulder, 'Thank you!' and 'Amen!'

Usually Laurel has a helper with her but she had come to Canberra at short notice. She told me later, 'I asked the Lord to please send me a God-fearing woman. Otherwise, bring me two ladies.'

Her second helper was my other bestie, Loretta. For when I longed to join the exodus to Canberra I answered a

Telegram post, 'Wanted Christian lady to share-drive Brisbane to Canberra, leaving early tomorrow.'

At an advanced age, I went on my first internet date!

A few texts, a five-minute phone call and I met my ride at 6am Wednesday. Her car was loaded with a tent, air mattresses, sleeping bags—all the gear I lacked. Strangers had provided cash for fuel and a cooler of nutritious food. She left her four children with their father to follow the call. We were besties within the hour.

Now, we felt uplifted to join the throng of flag-waving, singing, smiling citizens. The people-power atmosphere was electric. Mainstream media reported some thousands, but they were loose with the noughts.

Moses stood on a utility above a ROAD CLOSED sign. White-wigged and bearded, in white robes, he waved high a tablet inscribed: *'Exodus: Let my people go.'* This man flew into Canberra airport where taxi companies were forbidden to take fares to Parliament House. He had a staff. So he walked.

No politicians deigned to hear our protests but we marched in like-minded unity. A sign declared, 'Human Rights Come from God NOT Government.'

Outside Parliament House we sang *When the Saints* with improv makeshift brass and percussion. My only adverse symptom from four days' super-spreader event was a hoarse voice. Others fared worse.

Infiltrators tried to instigate friction with mainstream media at the ready. But we heeded advice to 'keep it nice'.

A euphoric crowd returned to Epic Freedom Camp where kitchen troops cooked meals for thousands. Food donations flowed in to feed multitudes. A huge street party of celebration evolved. People who were released from months of lockdown danced and sang. The Victorians especially were starved of community and hugs. Canberra lavished that. Some were jabbed, others not. Who asked?

After our exertions, we craved a Sunday sleep-in. But word went out... *Decamp.* The million campers must pack and leave. *Where?* At the rally space, divisive voices jostled for power. We heard of infiltration causing division, passing information to the police. Cops might move in. They did.

'First, move the vulnerable; elderly and single mothers with kids.' A 300-acre farm was ready with camp kitchen, facilities and portaloos. Police blocked entry. Some got in, but many were homeless, and had to relocate to other distant camping sites, with limited or no internet. That night Laurel sat from midnight in her car outside Epic Camp, praying while police moved in on the remaining campers. They arrested a man who asked a polite question.

Laurel rang me later. She'd stood reading Scriptures and praying on top of Red Hill, overlooking Parliament House where, she said, Satanic worshippers make sacrifices and curse our Peoples' House. God's voice told her, 'I will bring a sword into the Parliament House.'

I realised not only was I called that first day to facilitate her words, but also to write the inspiring story of her life.

Three years later, it's time to flesh out more information. We meet over fish and Asian greens in a Chinese restaurant. Bestie misses the food she remembers from the Torres Strait. 'It's not easy to eat healthy in the city.'

Laurel's life is a redemption story of how God empowered her to break free from three addictions: drugs; alcohol; and nicotine. Her early years on idyllic Boigu Island, Torres Strait, were nurtured by traditional elders and infused with Bible-based family and social cohesion. 'For me, growing up on Boigu Island was like heaven on earth,' she said.

From a baby Laurel was raised by her great-grandmother who was of the stolen generation. 'She was taken by force from Stradbroke Island where her white father swam ashore, escaping a ship from England. There he met a dark-skinned full-blood aboriginal and fathered mixed race children. One of them was my great-grandmother who was taken by force from her parents to Rockhampton and then to Bamaga in Cape York where she married a Boigu Island man.' After her great-grandmother died, Laurel was cared for by a grandmother, the daughter. 'I was brought up by grandparents, not parents.'

When Laurel moved to Thursday Island and Cairns for schooling, both were party places. Life spiralled downhill. By the age of 18 she typified the indigenous wasted-in-a-park lifestyle.

'God spoke to me through a night vision of hell,' she said. 'He told me that if I keep drinking I'll spend eternity in torment.' When she woke, Laurel sought out an Anglican priest and began studying the Bible. In Cairns she learned more from Pentecostal Christians. There, she also made hard-drinking friends.

'Whenever I got money, I'm drinking—strong drink like rum. You just feel miserable with no money, no nothing, that was the lifestyle I went through. Whenever I'm with my friends and they're smoking, I would smoke up to a packet a day. When I didn't have money, I'd look in the gutter for the cigarette butts. When I would smell the smoke, oh man, I'll just go buy a packet again and I was back at stage one again. If I saw a pub, I'd grab a drink, it was an open door for me.' For months, Laurel isolated and avoided driving past those lures until she was stronger and able to go back through those areas again.

'I had to do my part by saying *no* and isolating myself from friends who were smoking or drinking—physically remove myself from those temptation areas. My friends, who did way too much drinking and partying, were puzzled that I distanced myself. It was more than a year before I saw them again, after I was strong. When I went back, I felt sorry for them because they could never understand why I cut myself off from them. Now they realise why I stayed away—you must physically remove yourself from those temptation areas.'

Laurel made up her mind to change her life because of her kids. 'I only had two children back then. I didn't want them to be turning out like me. I'm glad I did make that change because they are now doing well. They're all in the workforce in indigenous communities. If I didn't change back then they probably would be into drugs and alcohol now. I was able to bring them up the right way—they've never seen their mother drink. It goes back to your mind. I was replacing alcohol with soft drink, bitter lemon or juice, getting my mind used to drinking healthy.'

'Habit,' I agreed. 'Sunset heralds wine o'clock. An hour working in my veggie garden delays that first drink. I set myself boundaries like *only with dinner*. But sometimes it's my go-to for stress release… before I seek God for strength. I realise that is a false refuge.'

Bestie offered to lay hands on me and pray for deliverance from alcohol.

She asked for deliverance from *all* alcohol.

I gulped. Jesus Christ wasn't teetotal. His first miracle turned water into wine. What about His final sacrament at the Last Supper before His body was poured out like wine? *Drink this in remembrance of Me.* But I hesitated to interrupt her flow. Can one brief an intercession hotline to heaven?

I didn't want to dishonour Bestie or her prayer. Worse, to dishonour God.

I bought a juicer, and that night I determined I'd go dry.

Bonus! The less I honoured wine-o'clock the more creative juices flowed. I prayed more when I retired fully *compis*. Channelled the voice of God into scribbles in the dark. Rustling notebook pages like a mouse to not disturb snoring husband.

The best ideas came just before sleep! They wove gossamer threads back-and-forth like spider webs. Once chosen, sobriety bore fruit. That thief in the night had stolen earlier creative ideas.

'Yes, you are winning,' Bestie reassured. 'He's a loving God but He doesn't want you to rely on your own strength, He wants you to rely on His, looking to Him.

Alcohol is a powerful temptation from which only God save. One day at a time.

'If I can do it, you can too,' reminded Bestie. 'When tempted, keep your mind occupied, with Bible reading, praying or watching a Christian movie. Change the negative to the positive. When you feel craving, just change it; I switched cigarettes for food. And if I put on weight I lost it eventually. It worked. Eat nibbles as well. Once you do your part you see miracles happen—especially when it comes to a stronghold.' She reminded me to pray, 'God, please take this away from me.'

Free from addictions, Laurel is a powerhouse for and with God. After completing courses in Mental Health and Aged Care, Laurel is studying to become a teacher. With a Bachelor degree she plans to bring Jesus' light into the darkness of indigenous communities.

She has preached for 25 years—all over Australia and also in Israel, Dubai, New Zealand, America and Greece (on Patmos where Revelation was written and Athens where Paul preached in Acts 17). Preaching has become hazardous, especially at the prolific protest marches. They are no longer peaceful.

'Please pray for me that there won't be any fighting. There's life-and-death situations.'

She told how 'Recently, I was in the city preaching with my megaphone. Two Muslim guys who passed, they chanted, "Allah Akbar!" They chant that before they do something to you. First time ever, since I've been out on the street twenty plus years, having this happen. Then after they disappeared along comes another Aussie guy—cause they'll use an Aussie to fight with you. This guy is screaming at the top of his lungs, coming towards me. Then another guy came racing from the traffic light saying, "Don't you touch her! Stay away from her!" I thought, *Wow, that's God. That must be an angel. He told the man to go away and then he left.'*

Laurel believes Australia is going away off the track and doesn't look like it's going to recover in a hurry. 'Christ's coming is very near and He's telling us to get ready. We must prepare ourselves, to walk in holiness and righteousness.'

Ten days after the horrific massacre of Jewish citizens at Bondi Beach, Laurel took a two-day bus trip to Sydney to share hope to a grieving community. Then on to Canberra where an FBI special agent repented of both his own sins and on behalf of the Australian government. This brave woman embraced terror zones in the power of the Holy Spirit.

While evangelising in Brisbane's night hotspot wilderness, Fortitude Valley, Bestie sometimes crosses paths with 'Moses.' Both are too engrossed spreading the news of salvation to hear each other's stories.

Whether preaching on the streets around the world or saving Gold Coast 'schoolies,' or in a shattered Bondi, Laurel praises God for her release from addiction. She invites people to also experience this liberation.

I'm privileged to call this brave spiritual warrior my bestie. And even more honoured that Laurel now calls me *yapa* which in her aboriginal language means closer than a bestie: *a blood sister*.

The Beauty of Broken Pieces

MIRANDA DE JAGER

1963. A small-town maternity ward in South Africa.

A newborn baby waited to hear her mother's voice. It had been gone for over a week. The nurses took good care of her, but how could they know about the seed of loneliness and rejection already sprouting inside? Once the adoption process was finalised, her new family picked her up.

Ilze was ten days old.

Five years later, her adoptive parents took her into the lounge and asked her to take a seat. 'Ilze, now you are a little older we need to tell you that you are an illegitimate child.' Ilze frowned at the unfamiliar word.

'When our baby girl died five years ago and we learned that we couldn't have any more children, we decided to adopt you.'

'Is my brother adopted too?'

'No, he is our own. He was five years old when you came to us.'

Ilze stared at her parents. *Does that mean I am not your own? Where do I belong? Where are my real mum and dad? Did they die? Are they in jail?* As she grew older, these questions hammered with ever greater intensity.

Unknown to Ilze, another young girl struggled with similar rock-hard questions that splintered her uncertainties into broken pieces hidden deep inside. It was 1975. I was nine. In my classroom, I'd wonder what was wrong with me. My school uniform was new and fitted well, I looked presentable and my grades were good. In fact, in the last quarterly exam I was the only student of the ninety odd kids in grade four to receive 100% in maths. Yet I had no friends. I sensed that others didn't like me.

Growing up, I often felt flawed. I struggled to talk and was unable to make friends. Mum said I was just shy, but it was only partially true.

Ten years later, I married and things improved a little because my husband made friends easily and invited them over. I enjoyed visiting and entertaining, even though I didn't talk much. At the age of thirty, I started studying and built a successful IT career. I worked full time, was involved at church and had lovely friends, but I never understood why I felt so small and unworthy.

Twenty-seven years later, I made myself comfortable on the plane for the last leg of our flight back to our new home in Brisbane. My husband and I had emigrated from South Africa to Australia nearly two years before and, while it was lovely to visit friends and family in South Africa, it was quite hectic. I was thankful, exhausted—and relieved to return home.

After dinner, I watched a movie. The drama of a woman with emotional problems due to past trauma captured my attention. The way she told her story, struggling to get the information out, triggered a deep reaction. A dizzy feeling at the back of my head was accompanied by unpleasant emotions. I stopped the movie to get some sleep but, when I closed my eyes, I had a brief flashback of myself as a little girl. I had never experienced anything like it before.

I knew I was small, about five, and there was someone with me in the forest close to my childhood house. It was so scary I took a deep breath to counteract the fear. The scene disappeared instantly. I knew what I saw, but the context and details eluded me.

Over the next few months I secretly tried to recover more memories. Without success. It bothered me so much, I eventually told my husband and decided to see a clinical psychologist. I prayed God would help me find the right person because the prospect was quite daunting.

By the Lord's grace, I found an experienced Afrikaans-speaking psychologist in our area.

It helped that I could relay my experience in my first language. She explained that dissociation is the brain's way of protecting us. Repressed memories are quite common with severe trauma. She taught me relaxing and breathing techniques—because the moment fear kicked in, the memories disappeared. During the next few months, I retrieved more memories and finally started to reconstruct the horrific events of my early childhood. Broken pieces that never made sense slowly started falling in place, yet I couldn't identify the perpetrator.

One morning a few months later, I woke up thinking not only about my shocking past but the mindboggling way the events were blocked from my memories. I never before realised there were gaps. I remembered the happy times with my family, all my school years, the names of my teachers and most kids in my classes but somehow my mind managed to block out specific traumatic events.

While I pondered, a new vivid flashback emerged. In it I was seven years old. The perpetrator was my father. I realised I'd known all along. Still, I was devastated. I guess I hadn't wanted to know. It didn't match the picture of the gentle Christian father I knew. It was so devastating. Was my entire life a lie? It was too surreal. Who was I?

In the weeks following, I cried constantly. At times suicidal thoughts entered my mind. I couldn't read my Bible and the Scriptures I used to quote felt meaningless. Yet I knew Jesus never left me. I still experienced His presence and His love carried me through.

While I struggled to come to terms with the truth, my psychologist was not surprised. In fact, she's suspected as much, but realised I needed to discover it for myself. I later recognised I was in denial, unable to believe my father's behaviour. I often asked my mother questions about my childhood but she insisted nothing happened. I desperately needed closure so I decided to try a different approach.

Sitting at my craft table one day, I paged through the beautiful scrapbook of our new life in Australia that I'd made for Mum and Dad. I slipped the poem I wrote to explain my emotions into the back of the album. I gift-wrapped it before sending it to South Africa. Being a poet herself, I hoped Mum would realise my distress and my desire to understand the truth. Dad confirmed receipt of the album and said Mom was typing a letter that he would email because she wasn't computer-literate. Waiting was excruciating. Why was it taking her so long?

A few weeks later, I held my breath as I opened Mum's long letter describing many little injuries I sustained as a child. Normal stuff, part of growing up. It was strange she had a few dates wrong because I knew from recent conversations she had not lost her knack for recollecting dates. I was shocked to read how the truth of a specific innocent event was twisted to exonerate my father. I clearly remembered what happened because I was twelve at the time. I felt sick to my stomach at the blatant dishonesty. Yet I thanked God for His wisdom and guidance. I had suspected my parents might lie so, while I told them I was haunted by newly discovered childhood memories, I was careful not to provide specifics. In my search for truth, I was hoping to compare their stories with my own memories. Sadly, Mum's response did not provide me with any new information, but it confirmed they knew exactly what I was referring to and were lying to protect their own images.

For two weeks, I mulled over the contents of the letter, devastated. How do I respond? Were they trying to make me think I was imagining the horror?

When Dad eventually asked if I'd received his email, I sent a short reply that often haunted me afterwards. I simply replied I received it but had no idea how to respond to all the lies. I said that I KNEW what happened to me but, if he did not want to talk about it, I would never ask again. When I clicked the send button, the strangest thing happened. The email gave a send error. I had to hit send three times before I received confirmation it had gone.

I didn't hear back from Dad. A week later my younger sister Venessa advised that he'd been taken into hospital with a heart attack. He needed a pacemaker and, while the operation was successful, he was kept in intensive care for observation.

Another week later, my mobile phone rang. It was Venessa, who never called due to the cost of international connections. Although I knew it had to be serious, nothing could prepare me for her next words. 'I am sorry, I have bad news. Dad died of another major heart attack in hospital.'

'How is that possible, I thought he was recovering well?'

'Yes, he was, it was quite unexpected.'

'Was anyone with him?'

'No, he was alone. I spoke to the nurses yesterday and they said he was improving.'

Shattered, my first thought was it was my fault because of the email. I had no words. With conflicting emotions, I thanked her for letting me know and said I would be in touch.

The next few weeks were a nightmare of decision-making as the oldest child. Family discussions were conducted on skype. Mom went into depression but, fortunately, Venessa was with her and handled the paperwork. During this time, Venessa discovered a letter, photos and birth certificate of an older sister we had not known existed. We decided to contact her, but I had so much on my mind I continued postponing.

It was several weeks later before I sat down in a comfy chair with my laptop. By that time, I realised that Dad's death was not my fault. My mind was finally clear enough to write to my new sister. I have read her first letter to Dad several times. Her words touched my heart and, while I knew Venessa had already written to her and they were waiting for me to write, they had no idea what I was dealing with. I needed to calm my thoughts and emotions so I could write her the beautiful informative letter I felt she deserved. I told her how I learned about her existence and provided some background on our life in South Africa, my career and our new life in Brisbane.

'We have a lovely house, supportive church family and many new friends.' I wrote about our last trip to South Africa and added I would love to hear from her.

This was the first of many letters and long-distance conversations between two sisters who should have grown up together. Ilze had only found her biological father—my father—two years earlier and had regular email conversations with both Dad and Mum until she mentioned it would be nice to meet them. At that point, Dad broke all contact without explanation. He simply changed his mobile number and email address. I can only assume he did not want Venessa or me to know about her. Sadly, our father rejected her twice. The first time was when he did not want to marry her mum, so her maternal grandfather forced her nineteen-year-old mother to give her up for adoption.

As we realised our similarities, Ilze and I grew close . Two girls who were forced to deal with life's raw reality at very young ages found solace in sharing our experiences. Ilze realised how much she was spared by growing up with a caring adoptive family. I found a soulmate who understood me, a caring older sister whose love helped me face the reality of past trauma.

We both realised that, by God's grace, we had become stronger and learned so much from what we suffered. What the enemy meant for evil, God has turned to good. When He heals our brokenness, His light shines through the cracks to reveal a beautiful mosaic, a mosaic planned by God since the beginning of time.

Uplifted Arms

RUTH BONETTI

$\mathcal{D}$id you survive a tough upbringing? Yes, it's relative. Remember the British comedy sketch *The Four Yorkshiremen?* In 1948 a pre-Monty Python quartet headed by John Cleese upped each other's ante of:

> *'…livin' in shoebox at middle of motorway'* with *'evicted from our hole in the ground.'*

> *'You're lucky. We lived in a rolled up newspaper in a septic tank. We hadta get up a'six in the morning, clean da newspaper, eat a crusta stale bread, go to work down the mill, for a 14 hour day…, and when we got home, our dad would thrash us to sleep with his belt.'*

> *'…our dad used to murder us in cold blood, each night, and dance about on our graves, singing hallelujah.'*

My teenage 'cardboard box' was flimsy, mushy from tears. Or a hole in the ground. Others did worse. I suffered verbal abuse, but not sexual. Neglect, but I wasn't dumped as a baby in a skip. But I struggled through my teens, riddled with self-doubt, low self-esteem, and insecurity. Minimal support from my parents who lived a distant thousand miles away, on a sheep property in western Queensland. Depression overwhelmed me as I struggled to iron my own uniform, make sandwiches and catch a bus to school—which I often missed.

I'm grateful to Glenice Palmer, working through Scripture Union, who uplifted me through those teenage years. Glenice spoke prescient words over me, that my gifting was in writing, even as I attempted to pursue a degree in Music, wherein lay my weakest flaws. With poor aural, rhythmic and harmonic skills, foundations were flimsy. History and English studies would have been a breeze but I chose music because my clarinet teacher listened to me, encouraged and supported me.

When he moved interstate, I felt bereft. During an emotional breakdown, I moulded from clay a downcast head circled by heavy arms around emptiness inside. Glenice gently unwrapped my arms. She fed me, tucked me in her spare bed, organised medical treatment. My tears emptied boxes of tissues. Glenice saved my feet from stumbling.

Fast forward a decade or two. Raising a family while juggling teaching and music commitments. Holding a household together.

Overwhelm submerged me. I needed escape. The perspective of sea horizons. These always uplift, courtesy of my Swedish Finnish heritage.

I reversed our second car out of the driveway past an anxious son. His brown eyes searched for reassurance. I hope I put my foot on the brake and paused? Said, 'Darling, I'll be back, promise. I just need sea air to revive me.' Many of his school friends lived in empty homes due to parental breakup.

I booked into the cheapest Caloundra accommodation our budget could afford. Tick; sea view but through ill-closing windows. Cross; nil security through dodgy door lock. How could I revive while feeling unsafe? I found another motel too far from the beach for salt air. In desperation, I rang a prayer supporter and poured out my woes.

'Ring this number,' she said. 'Joan offers her *Tranquillity House* to people in need.'

I drove off to a stranger near Tewantin. Joan hovered, ready to pray if asked. Served me nutritious meals, salads from her garden, garnished with nasturtiums. After a week in *Tranquillity House* I revived to return home to my family. To reassure the son who had feared if I would return. Did my hasty exodus signal a marriage breakdown?

In the thirty years since then, I have often phoned Joan to unburden. She has prayed powerful spiritual warrior prayers—that I have passed on to others whose lives hung by threads. Sometimes I would visit face-to-face. As she passed the seven-score-years plus twenty-two most of her ministry is by telephone. After which, every night she prays. for hours. Joan reminds me often that our family have a regular spot each night.

As thanks, I brought her copies of my books after they birth, grateful for her midwife support. Don't we authors know how arduous and painful is a book's process through its birth canal?

I gave her copies of *Midnight Sun to Southern Cross* and *The Art Deco Mansion in St Lucia*. Joan said her sister read the latter with interest for she had worked at University of Queensland. Perhaps I'd encountered her there in my student days? And she recognised many names of *Palette of Grace* authors. Both elderly, the sisters now live together.

Last year I brought around a copy of *Symphony of Grace*. 'Come into the kitchen and I'll make us a cup of tea,' Joan invited. In the kitchen we did double takes. The sister who had moved in with her is Glenice, the supporting angel of my teens. Over much of my life two sisters have upheld me in prayer. One on either side, each holding up an arm.

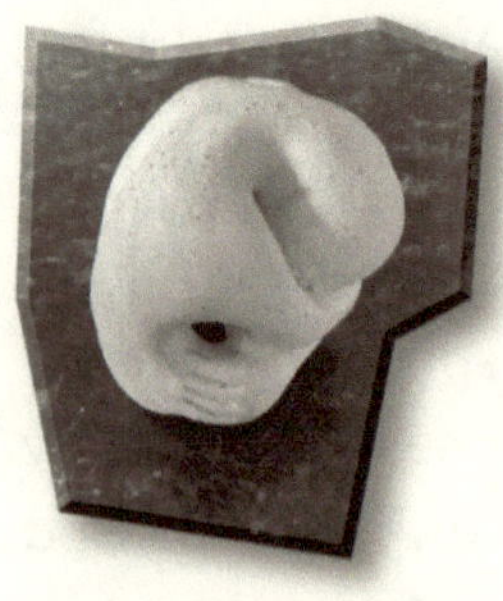

I thank God that He provided these two angel sisters who hovered around and behind me through my life. As each onion

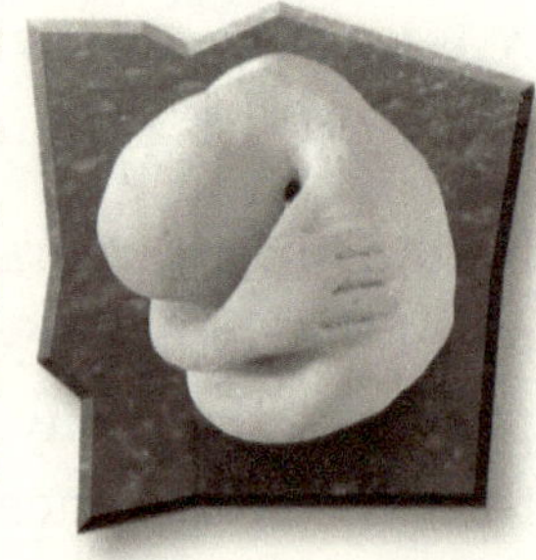

layer was torn off amid tears, they supported me to face and resolve issues, to move forward. And to in turn uplift others.

The Israelite army faced tough opposition from the fierce Amalekite army that far outnumbered them. But Moses encouraged Joshua to choose men and go out to fight.

'Tomorrow I will stand on top of the hill with the staff of God in my hands.'

As long as Moses stood and prayed, with arms lifted, Joshua and the Israelites gained the advantage against the enemy. When his arms tired the Amalekites won ground. So Aaron and Hur sat Moses on a stone and held up his arms, one on each side. His arms remained steady until sunset when the Israelites won the battle. A jubilant Moses built an altar and called it: THE LORD IS MY BANNER. He said *'For hands were lifted up to the throne of the Lord.'*

Happy ending, no? But… next chapter poor Moses was still struggling with overwhelm. He was worn out. Jethro, a Midianite priest and also Moses' father-in-law, came to share delight that Moses had played a leading role in God's rescue from Egypt. But noting that Moses sat alone as judge of the people from morning until evening he told him straight.

'The work is too heavy for you; you cannot handle it alone.' Delegate. Select capable men and have them serve as judges… have them bring difficult cases to you.

'If you do this and God so commands, you will be able to stand the strain, and all these people will go home satisfied.'

(Exodus 17:8–18:1–23)

Many of us try to fight our battles alone. No surprise that we flounder and tire.

We need others to uplift us. God, the burden-bearer, provides ways of escape. He sends friends, supporters and yes, angels to keep us from stumbling.

Humperdinck's *Hansel and Gretel* contains a beautiful Evening Prayer sung by frightened children alone in a forest:

> *When at night I go to sleep*
> *Fourteen angels watch do keep...*

I thank God for angels, both seen and unseen, who uplifted me through life's battles.

ESSAYS

Heartsease

ANNE HAMILTON

My favourite flower is the miniature edible pansy called the heartsease. A wildflower used in traditional herbal medicine, it has a striking cheerful face formed of five petals—two of a velvety royal purple and three of cream and canary yellow.

I had an entire garden bed of them once, bordered by rocks and a sprawling strip of alyssum, a froth of tiny white flowers that contrasted prettily with the heartsease. One day, as I was weeding and tidying up the riot of alyssum, I found a solitary heartsease in amongst the white foam, so well hidden I almost uprooted it before realising it was there.

Unlike regular heartsease with their vibrant violet and gold faces, this was difficult to spot as it was so pale it looked to have been blanched the same snowy colour as the surrounding alyssum. It was hoarfrost-white with just the tiniest dot of amber where the petals joined the stem.

I've always regretted not getting my camera out at that moment. But I thought I'd have weeks to snap a picture of this little gem and, anyway, it would be better to take a photo on a less overcast day. So I just smiled and reassured it: 'It's okay, little flower. Don't worry. You don't need to hide any more. I'm not going to pull you out. You're safe here.'

That was the last time I saw it. When I went back to continue gardening late the next day, I was stunned to find the little snow-white heartsease had vanished. There instead in its place in the middle of the alyssum, was a single stunning blue and lemon heartsease. Overnight, the flower had shaken off its anonymity, stopped blending in with its neighbours and dropped all effort at concealment. In fact, over the next two days, its colours deepened into the majestic purple and gold of its family beyond the alyssum patch.

I felt as if it had heard me. I felt as if it had responded to my reassurance of safety and that, free from any threat of danger, it had come to assume its real identity.

Is that too fanciful? Was it simply by random chance that a flower adapted to its environment by changing its hue so it wouldn't stand out… and abruptly ceased doing so just after I spoke to it? I like to think there was no coincidence involved.

Because I knew what that heartsease felt like… I didn't fit where I was planted. When I looked around me, I thought I was the problem. I was inordinately shy. I tried to live stunted, small, unseen, blending in—reducing my colours, acting as quiet as possible so no one would notice me. But then, when people overlooked me just as I'd hoped, I'd paradoxically feel disappointed at being left out.

This of course poses a question: if flowers can feel so threatened and unprotected that they adopt the colour of the environment they're in, how much more do humans feel the need to bleach out their true identity when they sense they are in an unsafe place?

I've been thinking a lot about the white heartsease lately, as I've pondered what aspect of love I value most. Lots of people choose unconditional acceptance and openly articulated affirmation, not just as the characteristic of love they most value, but as the only worthwhile one. It becomes their definition of love.

Now I couldn't care less whether you like me or not—just so long as you protect me. Protection rates far higher on the love scale than affirmation as far as I am concerned. Other people have made different choices in this regard—fairness and justice, for example, or presence not absence, are the pinnacle of their expectations around love. And if there's any conflict—as there often is—about which aspect of love is most important, well, I'm going to choose protection as my highest good.

After years of accusations about being 'negative' [*code*, I've come to recognise, for 'unloving'], I finally realised that my colleagues and I were really at odds about this highest good. Without protection, affirmation simply becomes toxic positivity. It's a form of valuing others, but without any real substance.

Nevertheless I pondered the question: should I give way? Should a protector defer to an affirmer?

I've wondered this because I've often felt under considerable condemnation about my so-called negative attitude. However lately it's dawned on me I should be paying more attention to a garden other than my own. I should be looking at the first garden: Eden.

God's assignment for Adam was to take care of that fertile and fragrant paradise on a mountain where four rivers had their headwaters. He appointed Adam as His first 'shomer'. This Hebrew word means *guardian, keeper, defender, custodian, steward, watchman.* Humanity's first and foremost job therefore is to *protect*. In fact, to fail to protect is to go the way of Cain who asked, 'Am I my brother's "shomer"?'

Strangely, protection isn't listed amongst the five love languages made famous by Gary Chapman—even though Paul's famous passage about love in his first letter to the Corinthians tells us *'love protects'*. It never mentions 'love affirms'. Nonetheless, curiously, the first listed 'love language' is words of affirmation. What are we to make of this anomaly? Are we to presuppose that the need for safety has been already met?

American psychologist Abraham Maslow's 'Hierarchy of

Needs' suggests that, once our basic physiological necessities are met—that is, food, shelter and clothing—then safety and security are what we look for next. We long to be free from fear, to not have to worry about threats, abuse or financial stress. We want protection—and it's so important to the average person that esteem, respect and affirmation run a distant fourth on the ladder.

It sometimes seems as if modern society has tipped Maslow's pyramid theory over, forcing it to balance on its tip. What do words of affirmation mean if they're not bolstered by action, and protective action at that? Like the believers that the apostle James admonished for saying to their starving, freezing friends, *'Be warm and eat well,'* but did nothing to help, affirmers need to move beyond words.

After all, affirmation might tell us repeatedly: 'You're valuable, you're worth treasuring, you're cherished,' but unless the message is backed by genuine care and active protection, there's no grounding in concrete reality.

I didn't ever tell the white heartsease in my garden that it was a precious treasure. The words, 'You're safe here,' said far more.

The unfolding of true identity happens when we feel safe.

Not before.

One Small Pebble

MICHELLE HOPE

What an eternal gift a kind gesture can give, and how it can create expanding rings of hope from a single pebble of compassion dropped into a pond of darkness. And often, the person who drops the pebble has no idea of the consequences of that one, simple act.

I had a phone call at the very lowest point of my life from someone I admire greatly, and I was completely taken aback to receive that unexpected call. The conversation we had literally saved my life, and I'm forever grateful.

Grace comes in many forms. Even a phone call. I was in the depths of despair, and had completely given up, but somehow after that conversation, I gradually pulled myself out of the inexorable, stygian abyss. I attribute it completely to the kindness of that wonderful person. And yet, the timing of that call can only have been prompted by God.

The person who phoned me knows who they are, and I thank them with all my heart.

And praise be to God, who sent me the help I needed when I was drowning in that bottomless chasm.

Promised Land

SONIA COUCHMAN

'Remove the sandals from your feet, for the place on which you are standing is holy ground.'

Exodus 6:5

*Q*ueensland. God's land. Land of Sunshine and Gold Coast beaches. Seamless stretches of coastline that sun-starved southerners watch though their television screens, longing for escape. Move further north where rugged folk wrangle cattle, while others tempt us with the delights of the Daintree. Perhaps a tropical island paradise is more your scene? Whatever the appetite, the far north of this great Southland can deliver on its promise.

These were the images I was raised on. Like Moses and the children of Israel crossing the desert, this 'Promised Land' was not on my 2025 radar. I'll admit that a journey north meant my own leaving, my own wilderness in pursuit of my own place to land. But any journey worth pursuing is never quite the children's story we've been taught, and certainly not the story I've spent my life teaching. My life's ministry was one of writing children's Bible stories and watching them come to life—in drama and song, all in pursuit of one question that haunts me still: what does it mean to follow? Now it was my turn.

It was mid-2024 when the offer came for my husband's work to move to Queensland—this vast desert of strange Australians I've now agreed to live with. I am a Melbourne girl. 52 years of being settled in an unpredictable cold, wrapped in a puffer jacket, hugging my keep cup of choice. I've been happy with that. What could be difficult about packing up a life, the kids, the cat, the car, and heading north? Everything, apparently.

It's not like I hadn't driven to Queensland before. We'd both been a few times, as kids—all through the 80s and 90s. As a young adult, I'd done the Gold Coast thing, more than once. I knew the Pacific Highway; how busy it would be over the Christmas season. This time, we had the luxury of travelling, just my husband and me, while we'd whisked children off to family in WA. We might even stop in Newcastle, visit hubby's sisters, test out a bakery, a Leagues club or three.

With our promised land plugged into the GPS, 140 boxes Brisbane-bound, life was in limbo. My father was never getting better; mum was worried, and my eldest was not coming with us. Nothing had prepared me for this. Every road in Melbourne, including its outskirts, had burned its place into my psyche as we dropped the cat off at his private airport. Early the next morning, the Hume opened up before us, and we were on our way.

In my mind's eye, I'd imagined children in the back seat, my sister and I with our red and orange clipboards noting populations of NSW country towns, a perfect distraction designed by my mother. Those towns, now an off-road option for the Australian driver, were replaced by the predictable multi-national roadhouses that drained our funds. Today I was the 'child' in the front seat, taking turns at the wheel, discussing fuel consumption with my husband.

Two days, four with the stops. That's all this trek required. The other side of Newcastle seemed strange and unfamiliar. The tolled roads were devoid of the romance I'd hoped for. And when the mobile signal cut us off from all contact, we relied on our backup compact-discs to transport us to easier days via 70s 'yacht rock' magic. Before long, our station wagon pulled into the car park of an oversized banana, and I was nine years old again.

But nothing is quite the same.

The tourists raced for free tables; it was hotter than I'd imagined, and the gift shop was awash with overpriced merchandise. The irony that I, too, was a tourist was not lost on me. Still, the lure of a chocolate frozen banana and pineapple milkshake was just the ticket to sugarcoat the last hours of a bittersweet journey.

The road in was slow, and the signs were weird to me, so foreign. Ipswich. Gold Coast. Toowong. The theme parks still stood, much as I'd remembered them, their metal skeletons raised to the heavens. I wanted to be repelled by it all. But I needed to live here now. Even as I messaged the children with the odd photo and commentary, no one seemed too taken by it. If surreal was an overused word, today I owned it. I was priming myself to say aloud, 'I am a Queenslander.' And it would be the most unsettling statement of all.

It was overcast at 5pm when we drove into our strange new surroundings. Our plants had survived along with the Christmas ham that we hoped might sustain us. Our final Melbourne Christmas had been the last of the lasts, for all sorts of reasons, and we needed something to remind us of that.

When the moving truck did arrive, the unpacking rhythm was the same. Bed assemblies, kitchen arranging, 1000 books to shelve. We are an academic pair living in an academic oasis, right here in this desert. As each item found its place, our new life—mine in its entirety, nestled itself into a standardised 1980s townhouse beside the smokestacks of a Queensland brewery. Not quite the burning bush I'd been on the lookout for all these years.

The odd colleague greeted us with wine and pleasantries. 'Welcome, take your time, you'd better get used to the weather,' the usual quips. Soon enough, the children arrived, along with the cat, and we settled into a lonely existence on the edge of the River City. You can be achingly alone, even in the midst of a well-established community.

We hopped about the surrounding churches, local markets, studied the bends of the river. We leaned into what we knew and what we had learned. Keep doing the same thing was the advice, look for the oasis in the desert, keep walking.

I knew little of Brisbane, her bridges, her strange houses being raised upon stilts after each torrential rain. At times, Coronation Drive reminded me of Albert Park, but I longed for the hum of the F1 cars practising while I lunched nearby in the gardens. There are new gardens now. The trees that surround my new quarters—the Dean's quarters in an Archbishop's paradise—have built their shade around me.

Who knew it would help? Certainly not me.

The new job that I had accepted gives me vantage across this new skyline. The six-minute commute to Mt Coot-tha allows me to watch the city as I work. I look out, locate our house, and watch the city at play or rest. I seek out the ugliest building on the Brisbane skyline, a subjective family game we've invented. For a moment I feel a kindred spirit with our favourite ugly Melbournian office tower. You do what you can to feel connected.

There were times we raced back to Melbourne, a PhD graduation, my father's failing health. Dad's decline peaked mid-year whilst my husband and I had snuck my eldest into Paris for a week enroute to her new life in the heart of London, chasing her teenage dream. Dad died in August. I made it just in time. I missed the big city on those trips, settling instead in the outer suburbs, making final arrangements, telling stories. I keep looking for a reason to go back, as if I could not just go back to see the people I love. I keep remembering my life is there.

Perhaps it is here now.

When October came, my feet still itched. Work was settling, the kids were settling, but I was rocky. 'You'll know it when we find it,' my husband said. I wanted to stay in the shade of this house, not venture out. Still, I knew I needed to feel an oasis beyond even this one. Something about belonging and place and being able to kick my shoes off and leave them at the door was niggling at me.

We pulled up at our new congregation a few weeks back. Things reminded me of home, a few of my homes. Our Melbourne parish, for one—a mix of eclectic folk who don't take themselves too seriously. We parked on the street. While I was a university undergraduate, I lived with my parents in an outer suburb of Melbourne, dense in bushland. For a moment, I was transported there. It was good. The first service was right, the liturgy un-seriously serious. We'd found it and I knew it.

For the last months, I've sung again at church. It's in my bag of tricks that's been stashed in the back of the cupboard, still not unpacked from the move. It had been over a year since I'd been able to sing. It was freeing. Two weeks later I read from Matthew's gospel, held it high and preached from it. The kingdom of God is near.

This was holy ground.

I lamented recently that I would not be in Melbourne for Christmas. But I will be home. My mother safely cared for by my sister. My eldest happily viewing the Northern lights with new friends. I will be here with a new family, sharing our Christmas table in this inner-city oasis. Hardly a desert. It's a place that I choose because today, this is what it means to follow. This vision realised of my personal Promised Land comes also with the promise of a decent Christmas meal.

You are welcome, and you can take your shoes off at the door.

Selah

God is trustworthy, reliable and all powerful
ROSEANNE HOLLIDAY

> *Life must be understood backwards…*
> *but… must be lived forwards.*[1]
>
> Soren Kierkegaard (1813–1855)

Kierkegaard's insight is true of me. The majority of my life has been lived as an undiagnosed autistic with co-occurring alexithymia, anxiety and recurring autistic burnout. Late diagnosis as autistic at fifty-two years of age, was followed by years of reviewing my life, identity and relationships with others, as well as analysing my Christian faith and practices.

---

1   Jack Madden, "Kierkegaard: Life Can only be understood backwards but must be lived forwards," *Philosophy Break,* October 2023, philosophybreak.com/articles/kierkegaard-life-can-only-be-understood-backwards-but-must-be-lived-forwards/.

This reflective essay explores some of my neurodivergent, autistic experiences and challenges which together with my faith journey have brought me to the place where I declare: 'Selah as a statement of faith in times of enduring stress,'[2] and acknowledge God is trustworthy, reliable and all-powerful in all circumstances of life. This is evident by His love and acceptance of neurodivergent autistic me, just as I am; I'm not broken and in need of curing. God valued every human being by giving His life and made the way even for me, to be included and to belong to His community of believers.

DISCOVERY... KNOWING WHY

Born neurodivergent, yet living life undiagnosed, my 'experience of disability' had been a slowly dawning awareness[3] that I was different from others. From my 2015 autism diagnosis emerged answers as to why my life and spiritual journey were different from others around me. Having always felt like a square peg trying to fit a round hole, I started to understand why I perceived myself as a misfit and judged myself as not good enough. The art of social camouflaging, of trying to blend in to be accepted, get things right and not be judged a failure were deeply embedded in

---

2   Elizabeth Lyon, "An Analysis of Selah in antiquity", (PhD diss., University of Birmingham), 2018: 244, etheses.bham.ac.uk/id/eprint/8625/1/Lyon18PhD.pdf.

3   Brian Brock, "What is Research on disability? Looking backwards to see Forward", *Journal of Disability & Religion*, 26:4: 393, tandfonline.com/doi/full/10.1080/23312521.2021.1912684#d1e121.

my psyche. Deep-seated fear of making mistakes and failure impacted my thought processes, decision-making and behaviours. Rejection sensitivity dysphoria in response to 'perceived rejection or failure can feel intensely emotionally painful, to the point that I [they] struggle with these feelings,'[4] especially when compounded by alexithymia, 'characterised by an impaired ability to be aware of, explicitly identify, and describe one's feelings.'[5] All of this had led to my being driven by performance anxiety and self-inflicted performance pressure to achieve acceptance by God, family and others.

PROFOUND REALISATIONS

Long before diagnosis, I repeatedly prayed for God to heal the difficulties experienced with regard to self-acceptance, anxiety, emotional processing, communication challenges and relationship breakdowns. One day I pondered, *'Love the Lord your God with all your heart, and with all your soul and with all your mind and with all your strength… love your neighbour as you love yourself.'*[6]

---

4   Amy Marshall Beb, "What to Know About Autism and Rejection Sensitive Dysphoria," *Very Well Mind*, February 05, 2023, verywellmind.com/what-to-know-about-autism-and-rejection-sensitive-dysphoria-7097539.

5   Jeremy Hogeveen & Jordan Grafman, "Author Manuscript: Alexithymia" (for *Handbook of Clinical Neurology*), HHS Public Access, 2022: 2, https://www.ncbi.nlm.nih.gov/pmc/articles/PMC8456171/pdf/nihms-1735580.pdf.

6   John 12:30–31 NIV

As I exited the car, a profound realisation dawned: 'How can I love others, when I do not love, accept or value myself?' My relationships were in turmoil, I was struggling in the workplace and pushing myself to keep performing at church, home, work and in the community. In hindsight, the toll of social camouflaging resulted in autistic meltdowns, shutdowns and burnout. This Scripture highlighted my need for self-acceptance.

ACCEPTANCE... VALUE

Psychological assessment revealed an autistic spiky profile of strengths and challenges, resulting in the misfit square-peg-round-hole paradigm being identified as the faulty lens through which I viewed myself. Just as God created biodiversity, neurodiversity continues to be part of His creative process. Therefore, 'if creation is good, as Genesis 1 repeatedly claims, then my neurodivergence [disability] is good.'[7]

Since I was 'formed in my mother's womb,'[8] God has always known and accepted neurodivergent, autistic, alexithymic, anxious me. This helped to reshape my perspective, accepting and valuing myself. I have started to fully appreciate that

---

7   Shane Clifton, "Crippling Christian Theology: Reflections of a post-Pentecostal disability theologian", *ABC Religion & Ethics*, December 05, 2020, https://www.abc.net.au/religion/crippling-christian-theology-disability-faith-and-doubt/12952958.

8   Psalm 139:13 NIV

God's love, acceptance and grace towards me is sufficient; it's His *'power that is perfected in (my) weakness.'*[9] However, as identified by Nancy Eiesland, a continued need for 'social change that would acknowledge our full value as human beings,'[10] requires me to acknowledge and accept my own value is not reliant on social expectations and limitations.

FAULTY LENSES

The phrase *'fear the Lord your God'*[11] appears multiple times throughout the Bible. Having performance anxiety issues and being prone to literal interpretation, I perceived God as being a 'black and white' rule taskmaster, constantly judging my actions as 'not good enough'. When the faulty 'autistic literal' lens was identified, recognised and challenged, a self-initiated exploration of Hebrew and English Bible translations began. Through meditating on Psalms 110–118, my literal interpretation of 'fear Jehovah, thy God'[12] shifted

---

9 2 Corinthians 12:9 NIV

10 (Eiesland, 2002, p. 13) in Deborah Creamer, "Theological Accessibility: The Contribution of Disability", by *Disability Studies Quarterly,* 2006, Volume 26, No. 4. dsq-sds.org/index.php/dsq/article/view/812/987

11 Deuteronomy 10:12 NIV

12 Deuteronomy 10:12 YOUNG'S LITERAL TRANSLATION

to a deeper understanding and recognition of 'revere your God'[13] and 'respect the Lord your God.'[14,15]

This challenged my often debilitating fear of failing God's standards as well as my faulty perception of Him as an authoritarian performance judge. My belief transformed to recognising God's love, mercy, forgiveness and desire for all people to be reconciled to Him and to each other. I have begun to better understand, comprehend and trust *'the breadth, length, height and depth of His love,'*[16] grace, forgiveness and compassion towards me.

PERCEPTIONS...

Socially naïve, literal, and overly trusting, I was often misinterpreted and misunderstood by others due to the 'double empathy problem'[17] of social communication mismatch between neurotypical and neurodivergent people. Delayed recognition of others' perspectives and misunderstandings by both parties, in addition to uncertainty

---

13   Deuteronomy 10:12, *The Contemporary Torah*, JPS, 2006,. sefaria.org/Deuteronomy.10?lang=bi&aliyot=0.

14   Deuteronomy 10:12 EXPANDED BIBLE

15   Deuteronomy 10:12 NEW CENTURY VERSION

16   Ephesians 3:16–19 NIV

17   Damien E.M. Milton, "On the ontological status of autism: the 'double empathy problem'," *Disability & Society* 2021, 27(6), 883-887, https://kar.kent.ac.uk/62639/1/Double empathy problem.pdf.

about how to repair and heal situations, negatively impacted relationship dynamics.

Just as Jesus' parable identified how the tax collector cried for mercy from God,[18] deep within me, I longed for God's mercy, forgiveness, healing, reconciliation and restoration of relationships—friendships where others would truly know and include me, rather than my social mask or my Christian performance façade. As I repeatedly sought God for guidance on relational restoration, a systematic pattern and process of forgiveness towards others and myself emerged, based on the prayer of the beaten, wounded, disabled, ridiculed, misunderstood Jesus for all human-kind when He hung on the cross.

PATTERNS... PROCESSES

The acute awareness of my need to *'not seek revenge or bear a grudge,'*[19] during my undiagnosed years meant the cry of crucified, dying, disabled Jesus on the cross: *'Father, forgive them for they know not what they are doing,'*[20] became my cry during relational challenges.

My expanded version became: *'Father God, forgive them for they know not what they are doing, saying or thinking and, Father God, forgive me for not knowing or understanding myself and what*

---

18   Luke 18:13 NIV

19   Leviticus 19:18 NIV

20   Luke 23:34 NIV

I was doing, saying or thinking. Help me to forgive them and to forgive myself. Help me to better understand them and myself.'

This process shifted my thoughts from reactive to cognitively responsive. I no longer took offence nor allowed anger to fester in my heart, mind or spirit. The forgiveness prayer progressively expanded to: *'Lord, I forgive them of their actions (i.e. attitude, behaviours, words etc.), I forgive them of the hurt their actions have caused me and I forgive them of the impact their actions and hurt have had on me.'* This same forgiveness framework guided the acknowledgement and confession of my actions, the hurt caused and the resultant impact my actions and hurt had on others and myself.

WOUNDS AND SCARS

Jesus' instruction to forgive others *'seventy times seven,'*[21] has required repeated implementation of the forgiveness process. This has not meant the hurts or impacts have been forgotten; rather wounds have healed and sensitive scars start to fade. Though the emotional trauma scars may continue to be prodded or split open by myself or others, I know the emotional healing recovery journey of forgiveness is ongoing.

---

21   Matthew 18:22 NCV

Just as the Apostle Paul discovered when he pleaded for healing of *'a thorn in his flesh,'*[22] I need to rely on God's help and strength in my distress, brokenness and weaknesses. I am no longer emotionally crippled by frustration, anger, regrets, bitterness, or the need for revenge and vindication. I have been set free to live authentically as an autistic woman, able to grow in understanding of God, myself and others.

COMPASSION...

Repeated episodes of stress, distress and autistic burnout have continued to impact my self-perceptions. Practices of being still through recognising, mediating and reflecting on Scriptures about God's trustworthiness, reliability and all-powerfulness have enabled me to acknowledge my ongoing struggles.

My initial 'go to' verse was: *'Be still and know I am God.'*[23] When my gaze expanded, I recognised the wider core themes of Psalm 46 to trust in God in all life's circumstances.

Selah, an untranslatable Hebrew word after verses 3, 7 and 11, caught my attention.

Psalm 46:1–3 spotlighted my need to trust God as an *'ever-present help in trouble.'*[24]

---

22   2 Corinthians 12:7b–10 NCV

23   Psalm 46:10 NCV

24   Psalm 46:1 NIV

Verses 4–6 reinforced dependence on God's reliability: '*God is within me [her]*'[25]—fitting with Jesus' promise '*the Spirit of truth… lives with you and… in you.*'[26]

Finally, the repetition of *Selah* reinforced the trustworthiness, reliability and all-powerfulness of God: '*The Lord Almighty is with me [us], the God of Jacob is my fortress. Selah*'[27]

STEADFAST FAITH

Everyday challenges both pre- and post-autism diagnosis have led to a deeper faith, trust and reliance on God. My past has been reframed by accepting and valuing my differently wired brain. Self-compassion has emerged regarding the impact of neurodivergence on my life. Forgiveness towards myself and others has become grounded in the forgiveness Jesus demonstrated whilst dying on the cross for *everyone*.

Selah, the unknown Hebrew word 'found seventy-one times in the Psalter and three times in the Book of Habakkuk,'[28] has become a signpost, a stillness reminder to stop my striving and notice the faithfulness of God in all of my life circumstances, interactions and challenges.

---

25   Psalm 46:5 NIV

26   John 14:15–17 NCV

27   Psalm 46:7, 11 NCV

28   Elizabeth Lyon, (2018), 242

BIBLIOGRAPHY:

Beb, Amy Marshall, 'What to Know About Autism and Rejection Sensitive Dysphoria,' *Very Well Mind,* February 05, 2023, verywellmind.com/what-to-know-about-autism-and-rejection-sensitive-dysphoria-7097539 (accessed 12.06.2024).

Brock, Brian, 'What is Research on disability? Looking backwards to see Forward', *Journal of Disability & Religion,* 26:4, 390-413, doi.org/10.1080/23312521.2021.1912684 (accessed 05.06.2024).

Clifton, Shane, 'Crippling Christian Theology: Reflections of a post-Pentecostal disability theologian', *ABC Religion & Ethics,* December 05, 2020, abc.net.au/religion/crippling-christian-theology-disability-faith-and-doubt/12952958 (accessed 12.06.2024).

Creamer, Deborah 'Theological Accessibility: The Contribution of Disability,' *Disability Studies Quarterly,* 2006, Volume 26, No. 4, dsq-sds.org/index.php/dsq/article/view/812/987 (accessed 05.06.2024).

Hogeveen, Jeremy & Jordan Grafman, "Author Manuscript: Alexithymia" (for *Handbook of Clinical Neurology*), HHS Public Access, 2022, https://www.ncbi.nlm.nih.gov/pmc/articles/PMC8456171/pdf/nihms-1735580.pdf (accessed 14.06.2024).

Lyon, Elizabeth, "An Analysis of Selah in antiquity", (PhD diss., University of Birmingham), 2018, etheses.bham.ac.uk/id/eprint/8625/1/Lyon18PhD.pdf (accessed 05.06.2024).

Madden, Jack, "Kierkegaard: Life Can only be understood backwards but must be lived forwards," *Philosophy Break,* October 2023, philosophybreak.com/articles/kierkegaard-life-can-only-be-understood-backwards-but-must-be-lived-forwards/ (accessed 25.05.2024).

Milton, Damien E.M. (2021). "On the ontological status of autism: the 'double empathy problem'," *Disability & Society,* 27(6), 883-887, kar.kent.ac.uk/62639/1/Double empathy problem.pdf (accessed 07.06.2024).

The Contemporary Torah, JPS, 2006, sefaria.org/Deuteronomy.10?lang=bi&aliyot=0.

The Expanded Bible, Copyright © 2011 Thomas Nelson Inc.

Young's Literal Translation, 1898 Baker Book House, Grand Rapids, Michigan.

Moving In

PAMELA JULIAN

'Jesus answered: When a person really loves Me, they will keep My word (obey My teaching); and My Father will love them, and we will come to them and make our home (abode, special dwelling place) with them.'

John 14:23 AMP

*G*od has accepted your invitation—Father, Son and Holy Spirit—and He's moving in. Note—*moving* in, not *have moved* in. It's ongoing; a lifetime of transition.

No longer is it just your home now, but a shared dwelling. They will *make* their home with you—again, an unfinished transaction. There will be changes, painful at first, but you'll adjust. In fact, you'll come to like it.

They like open-plan—no hidey holes, no secret spaces. The light shines into every corner. It might require some renovations—changing doorways and windows to make it bright and open, clean and stream-lined. But how fresh it will be. So uncluttered. So free.

Your relationship with God—it's not what you thought. He wants more—not just a space when it suits. A corner of the loungeroom? The spare room? He is big; so much bigger than the space you made for Him. The whole house can't contain Him.

And now there's a whole new focus for your home. Cleaning out old junk. Furniture gets moved around; some gets tossed. He brought beautiful things to place in your home—new linen, exquisite china. Will you make room? Or cling to your old favourites? God won't trash your home, just gently and persistently prod you to clean out junk; keep only things that remind you of your worth to Him.

'You don't need this—it can go.'

'Oh, but it was special... once.'

'Once, but not now. You have Me now. I'll satisfy those hollows, those empty places where you stuffed things to fill the void.'

'We'll move it out together. Laugh with Me as we clean it out. Enjoy Me, be filled by My Presence here with you. Let the past go and look forward to the future. I'll always be here—I won't leave you. You'll never have this emptiness that needs something to cling to, stuff to fill it. I won't leave your home—*our* home—hollow, barren, but rich and full.

'The changes to your home will make it more you, not less you. Don't be afraid that you'll lose yourself. You can't be whole without Me. You can't be the sum of all your parts unless I bring them together and empower, yes, empower you, to be all that you were meant to be. You won't lose yourself, but rather find more of yourself than you ever thought there could be.

'I've put the kettle on. You grab that box of old keepsakes that you can't bear to part with. Here, sit on the sofa, hold My hand, and we'll go through it together.'

POETRY

Set Free

REBEKAH ROBINSON

There are latches
    and padlocks and deadbolts
        and twisty-turny chained knots
    some of them,
        like an invisible force field until
you plough headlong into them
        and think, *where did that come from?*

Some great gleaming gates impose,
        topped with paling barbs
            to blench the brightest soul.
Some are nondescript little boxes
        which quietly refuse to give.
Some are yokes which went on easily enough
        but won't come off again.

And so,
    there are keys.
        Faith will unlock grace,
        and grace provides the faith.

            But wait! There's more.

Because keys are not always metal.
Sometimes, they are easy listening.
    Instrumental.
    Choral.
And we can make a beeline to see
    the delightful, easy effervescence
        of genuine emotion.
    Life does not have to be flat.

Some keys are plastic-tipped, rowed over crumbs
    from past ponderings,
        sticky with late latte
        and lateral ideas.

Our most valuable assets
    may be unlocked not by imposition
        but by a gentle squeeze
        from across the room.

And some things only open up
     when we gently
          tap out,
          letter by cautious number,
               the price we're willing to pay.

One holds all the keys.

They are written into
     the fabric of His Word,
          the faithful penning
          and pining of His melodies,
     the treasure hidden in the field
          of communion with Him.

          Faith will unlock grace,
          and grace provides the faith.

And when the barred door swings wide,
     walk through it.
And if your legs or your heart fail you,
     if the shackles broke you,
          know the victory parade
          might continue down the street
     but He will come back for you.
Always and without fail.

I'm a Heretic
MERRIDY GLAZEBROOK

Maybe we're all slightly dodgy
With our theology
Maybe we've all said some stuff
That just ain't true
Maybe we're all heretics
Maybe it's hereditary
That we'll mess up
When we talk about You

Yet I still choose to believe
That You're working here
You don't need my perfect speech
To be changing lives
One day we will see
With our own eyes
And I think that being wrong
Won't matter as much
As being by Your side

Can I trust in Your heart
Even when I can't see the path
Can I live in hope
That You'll teach me what I need to know
Can I live with the belief
That You are all I need
And my theology may be slightly dodgy still
my theology may be slightly dodgy still
after all, I'm a heretic.

Call to Prayer

LINDA BARTON

I feel the dread
At the thunderhead
Agitating on the horizon,
With despising voices crying
Retribution.

Ripped and rent
Bullets and hatred spent
Nation of heavy hearts
Godhead torn apart
Mourning.

Religion as division
Activism and circumcision
Notions of brotherhood
Crucified and misunderstood
Derision.

Mourners with heads bent
Hearts bleeding lament.
Shrouded figures unbowed
Parting the crowd.
Resolute.

Call to prayer
Voltaire in the air.
Forgiveness of sins
Carried on angel wings
Harmony Day.

Wondering and Pondering
ROSEANNE HOLLIDAY

Change of life circumstances came suddenly. Repeated trips to hospital and my husband's health hit the point where I could no longer juggle working and caring. I was burnt out. Though I tried to control the transition from being in the workforce to being home full-time, I struggled.

Soon after, another change was forced upon us. A vacate notice from our landlord brought the news that we needed to find somewhere new to live. For months, I had sensed an urge to pray for housing stability and security for our future. Now, urgency was in our prayer. A suggestion was given. A door opened for us to acquire a forever home within a retirement village. When we moved in, I was just turning sixty. I didn't see myself as old. Again, I struggled as reality struck me—I am now a senior.

One year later, whilst holidaying in southwest Western Australia amongst the tall trees of Pemberton, I wandered past a fallen tree. I started wondering and pondering the massive adjustments, changes and growth that had occurred. New seasons of life take time and I am still a work in progress. Ecclesiastes 9:4a ISV reminded me, *'While someone is among the living, hope remains.'*

The grace of God continues to ground my being and guide my way as I adjust, grow and flourish in this new season of changing life roles and circumstances. Softly whispered prayer became: 'Lord, may I be faithful in producing seeds of hope, just like the toppled black wattle tree bursting forth with yellow joy-filled blossoms hoping to spread seeds and see new life emerge…'

Old Tree…

Old tree toppled
Uprooted by the storm
One year on
Exposed severed roots
Pointing heavenward
Deep faith roots holding firm
Growing stronger, drawing sustenance

Old tree altered position
Changed life conditions
Perspectives requiring adjustment
Scarred trunk, mosses thriving, lichen spreading
Twisted blackened limbs budding
Fresh green leaves emerging
New growth seeking light

Old tree responding
Seasons changing
Refreshing showers of rain
Warmth of spring
Coloured blossoms opening
Perfumed air attracting insects
Potential development... a multitude of seeds

Old tree, reinvigorated
Purpose renewed
Faith restored
Mind, body, heart and spirit regenerated
Acceptance, connection and belonging reframed
Desire to grow, thrive and inspire re-established
Seeds of faith, hope, love, joy, peace and grace reproducing.

Changed for Go(o)d

MIRANDA DE JAGER

Like a portal opening slowly
Fragmented pictures taunted me
Out of sequence, confusing
Glimpses of a past lost in time
The portal widened gradually
Revealing the shocking truth

Gazing into my past
Bravely absorbing the secrets
Changed everything forever
Gone were the illusions
Family cover-ups, fairytales
Replaced by disgrace

If merely facts surfaced
It would be more bearable
But painful emotions
Buried for decades
Returned with vengeance
As each memory unfolded
It crippled my inner being

Yet through it all
My Heavenly Father never left me
He was there to pick up the pieces
Hold me, guide me, and protect me
He healed the wounds one by one
Restored my image, my confidence
He turned brokenness into beauty

Into Silence

PAMELA JULIAN

You have taken account of my miseries;
Put my tears in Your bottle. Are they not in Your book?

Psalm 56:8 NAS

The ceiling is thick,
dense.
No words rise
as incense;
they stick;
unspoken,
linger on my tongue.
Each wound added
forms a laminate,
while tears fall—upward—
dissolving small holes
in the silence.

Until—
Your head bowed
over Your cupped hand
eyes tenderly counting
each tear drop
now resting in Your palm
a precious salt-water pool.

A Seasonal Meditation

JUSTIN YEEND

A poem inspired by the book, *Heart and Mind:
The Four-Gospel Journey of Radical Transformation,*
by Alexander John Shaia

*T*his poetic meditation tells the story of an individual's radical journey of faith from a first encounter with God to being part of a church community. Winter starts as the narrator experiences a dark night of the soul and encounters God for the first time through an existential crisis. This season comes to an end as the narrator encounters God as the light amongst the darkness. Spring commences with tears of joy at this first encounter with God. Spring is an expression of revelling in the joyful experience of being born again in God's presence and the awe of God's creation. This season concludes with God leading the narrator to an indigenous community who tell stories of the carpet python.

The mosaic is a symbolic and inclusive reference to both Moses and the bronze serpent (Numbers 21 and John 3) and its significance for healing and Christ's salvation. During summer, God guides the individual along a path of possibility and connection with other people, particularly amongst the diversity of unheard voices. This season is about God steering the narrator to transition from an individual experience of grace to embody God's divine image and transform others through community connection. Finally, Autumn commences with the narrator as part of a faith community that supports and struggles together as they encounter the next life crisis collectively.

Enduring Mark's Winter Storm

You found me
When the days were short and cold
And black clouds tempered the horizon.
For darkness taunted me like an unseasonal storm

You stood secure
When a sudden wind arrived
And shuddered the blinds with a rattle and hum
For the draught stirred my sleep like an uninvited guest

Your eyes shone
When fierce gusts shouted angrily
And my vacant rooms echoed an ominous silence
For the mansion you built could withstand the deluge

Your lips parted
When the eye of the storm lingered
And dappled lights pierced my broken windows
For your rainbow breath is woven through shattered glass

Resting in John's Spring Garden

Your voice echoed
When clouds softened and sighed
And tranquil puddles danced across my roof
For rain drops wept from eaves like a gift of tears

Your arm outstretched
When the sun was bright and gentle
And flame trees boasted a fiery canopy
The flowers glowing like an imperishable longing

Your hands guided
When the wind was cool and brisk
And Honeyeaters thrived in Silky Oak streetscapes
For your garden sings like an orchestra of reverence

Your brush poised
As your ambience tinted blue heavens
And traced my friends across Gubbi Gubbi lands
For the carpet python glistened like a bronze mosaic

Walking Luke's Summer Road

You and I strolled
When the days were long and hot
And the arid road shimmered with a mirage
For your garden flourishes like wildflower in dry soil

We meandered
As lorikeets wove through the rainforest
And their feathers painted a palette of pure joy
While singing a symphony of harmonious praise

We waded
As shady creeks whispered
And the forgotten held their breath in awe
In gentle streams that feed loneliness with hope

We searched
As the sun scorched and shimmered
And the sky resounded with unheard voices
Seeking connection through a kaleidoscope of stories

Climbing Matthew's Autumn Mountain

In congregation we climbed
When the air was cool and crisp
And white clouds lined the mountaintop
For the steep incline tested our endurance

We cried together
When the air became thin and colder
And we hungered for the forest below
For your voice encouraged us to move forward

We persisted together
When the winds became heavy
As the poor were elevated by strong hands
For your will was written into our hearts

We breathed together
When the summit was silence and awe
And the mist became a blanket of faith
For we were ready for the winter ahead

With You

MERRIDY GLAZEBROOK

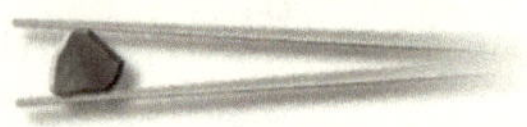

Can I come to terms with the fact
I may never come to terms with it
Can I work it out so that
I'm ok working it out with Jesus

All these burdens I took for my own
All these stone walls I took to calling home

But You came to break down my walls
Show me Your face
Let me see Your face
And my towers that were way too tall
Were washed away
In Your amazing grace

I thought the end was to be perfect
You showed me You are the end

I'm letting go of false perfection
I'm letting You change my perception
I live this life in tension
But I live it with You
I live it within You

Fringe Benefits

RAELENE PURTILL

When the ruddy fluid which animates our
    corporeal beings remains,
it is life,
warm, pulsing, generous life.
But to leave, to leave the body, is death.
To exit a wound and spread out cold,
to cry for revenge through the years
from where it left the first murdered corpse,
to that which flows regularly until we are old,
when blood leaves the body, it is to death.

Why are we the ones who bleed?
Is it because we are the ones who sacrifice?
Because we are the ones who give up our bodies
When we offer them to others' needs?

There is power in our bodies.
Potentially our frames bear life,
but life that comes from our body, brings death too,
and my body was assigned to death.
Life and death played out their existential rage
within and without of me.
The blood cycled back and returned
like a wave with a will of its own.
What should have meant life,
instead, meant death to me.

The doctors did not know.
They did not want to know.
But they knew the fear of ancient rule.
Their dread and past observance,
prevented them and prohibited me.
So, they were quick, so quick,
to call me impure.

Oh, they took my money,
they took everything I had
and then they took everything I was
and declared me unclean.
Not unwell, not in need,
but unclean.
Set apart.
Everything was gone.
All.

Except the blood,
for twelve years.

Then came the day the Teacher arrived
'The Teacher's in town,' the cry went about.
Could I remain unseen if I went out?
That was the day I contrived a plan
to touch the hem of His robe.
To steal my cure was all I had left.
Concealed in the crowd,
No one would know of my theft.
That was the day I had decided.
That was the day that my need collided
with Him.

So, there I was trembling at the tassels,
reaching for the rim of His robe.
Unhinged at the fringe
hanging at the horizon of my hand.
I touched that knotted cord,
tagged the tassel,
rubbed up against the robe, and
felt the fringe.
My need forged its way through my fingers,
and connected, like the arcs of a circle.
My blood for His coming sacrifice.
His bleeding for my healing.

'Who touched Me?' He asked.
The disciples laughed,
'It could have been anyone.'
He said, 'I felt My power.'
And I wanted to cry out
'So did I. So did I.'
But I continued to cower.
'Who touched Me?' He asked.
And the crowd parted,
like the Red Sea
and there was the Teacher
looking at me!

Twelve bloody years evaporated.
The death in my body was replaced by life,
warm, pulsing, generous new life.
The blood in my body
returned to its place.
In the moment I came to Him
face to face.

So that is my testimony,
the story I tell.
The word from my Lord,
'Go in peace, your faith has made you well.'

Based on Luke 8:40–43

FICTION

Fragments of Obedience

or *Scenes in Stone*

LINDA BARTON

The hall was cooler than the streets, shadows stretching across patterned stone. Outside, morning pressed against the shutters; inside, the air held steady—burned resin, oiled cedar, the faint metallic tang of arms. Beneath your sandals, the floor was a shimmering sea of colour. Up close, each tessera was only a chipped fragment: dull red, fleck of lapis, shard of limestone. Meaningless fragments. Step back, and lions leapt into form, vines curled, waves unfurled. The whole was made of pieces too small to name. You noticed, as always, how close your duty kept you to fragments, how little of the whole ever touched you.

You stood to the right of the dais as assigned, spear in hand. The wood fit your palm from long use, polished smooth where your fingers always rested. Herod Antipas leaned forward on his chair, rings glinting as he toyed with them. Carved cedar panels swallowed echoes, and the lower walls bore mosaics—bright markers of wealth and privilege. The floor never changed, though the men who walked it always did. You reminded yourself that soldiers were like tesserae, their service pieces of something greater.

He entered—not in chains, but ringed by watchful eyes. A Galilean. His robe was plain, torn and blood-stained. He'd obviously received a beating before being brought here. Most prisoners scanned the room, measuring exits, seeking allies. Not him. His gaze did not ask. It seemed to rest in the space without pressing against it. You noticed, then told yourself not to.

The chief priests and scribes followed, words beginning before their sandals stopped. Accusations stacked, each voice laying another tile in a picture they wanted the tetrarch to see: stirring up the people, teaching everywhere, trouble from Galilee to here. Herod's mouth curved, pleased and curious, like a man promised a spectacle.

'So you are the one I've heard about,' he said, loud enough to carry. 'Show me a sign.'

Laughter in the back of the room was anticipatory, not yet cruel.

The man said nothing. Silence stood in the centre of the room like a stone no one would lift. Herod tried again—words half-invitation, half-trap. The priests pressed harder.

Still the Galilean was quiet. He did not drop his eyes, nor fix them on Herod, nor sink them into the floor. He looked at people, one by one, as if each were a single tessera in a pattern only he could see clearly. When his gaze touched you, no plea rested there, nor accusation. Something stranger: a steadiness that suggested you were already known. You felt a tremor of your own fragility, worthiness, start to take root.

A gesture from an officer, sharp but wordless. 'The robe,' he added after you had already begun to move. The chest opened on purple wool, soft and heavy, the kind that speaks authority without a word. You carried it back and draped it over the Galilean's shoulders.

The cloth fell well, as though made for him. A murmur swelled into hard laughter. Heat rose at your neck; you clamped your jaw. Every chuckle pressed against your spine, reminding you of a part of yourself already surrendered. Mockery was ordinary, part of the order of things: rank crowning rank, the show of power. It kept men alive in this hall.

Yet ordinary did not close the thought that opened in you like a door you hadn't seen until your foot struck it. You saw again the floor's fragments—how near you always were to them, never knowing the whole. Duty, too, was meant to be a picture: you at your post, spear ready, obedient, in the place assigned. Step back far enough, it should resemble honour. Today, the picture trembled while laughter shook the air at your ears.

Herod's curiosity thinned in stages, like a lamp guttering as oil ran low. He asked, and received nothing. His eyes hardened, his mouth flattened. The priests clamoured; their voices broke and fell like waves. You had learned the music of power: the pitch that meant boredom, the hush that meant decision. Herod leaned back at last.

'Send him back to Pilate.' The words shifted everything into motion again. Hands turned, sandals scraped. The purple robe remained on him. That, too, was part of the message.

As he passed your post, his eyes caught yours. Not pity. Not blame. Only the same steady recognition. You made your face stone. If there was a picture hidden in this day, you could not yet see it. But your own reflection in that gaze struck like a shard: you had followed orders, yet in the obeying, something of yourself had been left bare, exposed to every eye, including your own.

When the chamber emptied, quiet returned all at once, the trained silence of a hall used to command. When your gaze finally dropped, the mosaics were unchanged: lions hunting, vines winding, waves breaking. A soldier learns to let such things pass like smoke from a lamp hole. Yet today, shame clung to your shoulders heavier than your spear, heavier than obedience. You repeated the truth drilled into you: had you acted differently, you'd be dead already; your roof marked; your name, small as it was, diminished to nothing. You repeated it until it sounded empty.

You thought of the Galilean's silence. Men stayed quiet for many reasons: fear, calculation, disdain. His quiet had no scent of any of those. It had felt like a stone set in exactly the right place, not a stone that refused to move. That was the part you could not sort, and the not-sorting pressed against you.

You remained at your post until reassigned to relieve the guards at the entrance gate to the complex. Outside, the light had gone harder. Traders' voices bounced from the walls, streets thick with bodies pressing in currents you had to lean through to reach your post. From the praetorium, the noise swelled—a roar that meant a verdict was being steered. In the crowd you recognised men from your childhood, men you had arrested, men who never looked up from their stalls. All pieces jostling into a shape you did not want to see.

In a side street, a boy bent over a broken tile, tracing the crack with a stick. His mother tugged his sleeve, urging him on, but he resisted without looking up. You remembered yourself at that age, already cataloguing danger in faces, already learning how to shape your expression into neutrality, how to become a fragment unnoticed. You had always called it wisdom. Today it felt like a habit grown too small, insufficient to protect what remained of honour.

By late afternoon, word thinned, then hardened: the governor would have his way. No one said it plain, but the knowledge ran under speech like mortar under stone. Later the stories would grow edges. For now, only the crowd's roar carried, weight pressing into the ground. You stood aside as soldiers passed, escorting the Galilean bowed beneath a wooden beam. The murmur followed—anger mixed with awe. Your orders did not join you to theirs. You stayed where you were set, because that is how patterns hold. Yet the awareness gnawed at you: patterns endure, but pieces can be flawed.

At evening your watch ended and you made your way back to the barracks. The courtyard lay quiet, the well at its centre ringed with worn stone. A lamplighter moved along the perimeter of the palace complex, flame flickering in a wire basket, touching wicks into glow. Evening burned down to embers. You sat on a step, helmet beside you, listening to the city's breath. The noise from the northwest had faded into something you could not name, not silence and not sound. You told yourself you had done your duty. You told yourself again.

At your side stood a basket once filled with tesserae for repairs. Only a few remained: flawed cubes, offcuts, shards whose colours matched nothing. You reached in and drew out a square of dark blue. Alone, it looked like nothing—neither sea nor cloak nor eye. In the hall it could have been any of these. You rubbed away mortar dust, set it on the step, heard its faint click.

You thought again of the Galilean—his silence not refusal but placement. It mattered where a man set himself, and why. You had not set yourself anywhere today, except where commanded. That had been survival. It had not been enough. The weight of it pressed on your chest like a missing tessera in a larger pattern, a reminder that some failures could never be repaired.

When you rose, you carried the empty basket to the well, left it where it could be found again. You lifted your helmet, brushed dust from its rim. The city breathed in, breathed out. The mosaic of the hall would look unchanged at dawn—lions, vines, waves. Up close, the parts would remain hard to read. From far enough away, someone would see the picture and know its meaning. You did not know if you ever would.

Your sandals struck stone as you walked away, the small, ordinary sound carrying with you into the narrowing dark, piece by piece. Each step felt heavier than the last, as if the weight of the purple robe clung still to your shoulders. You had obeyed, yet obeying had hollowed you. The pattern of duty remained, intact and whole, but you could see only the cracks—your failure laid bare in the silent judgment of your own eyes. The hall would remember nothing; the lions and vines would hunt and wind as they always had. You, however, carried the mosaic of shame, each fragment pressing into your chest, a reminder that honour could be stripped even when the law was obeyed.

Based on Luke 23:8

In the Basket

LEXIA MACKIN

'All right, class. Settle down.'

Mrs Mac was my grade two teacher. She was so nice. I was excited to come to school today because I had something to tell in *Show and Tell*. Something big. Usually nothing happens in my life but something big was going to happen and I wanted the whole world to know. Well, *my* world, anyway.

'My mum told us last night we were having a baby. But we won't see it for another five months and I can't wait to see it. I'm hoping it will be a baby brother.'

'Thank you, Miriam. *Show and Tell* is over now, so take out your homework books and open to last night's homework.'

As I walked home with my friend, Tiana, I told her that Mum didn't know if it would be a boy or a girl but I don't see how she doesn't know. If she knows she's having a baby, why doesn't she know that? It doesn't make sense to me.

Life went on a usual. Button and I did our jobs around the house. Loui did hers but she didn't have as many jobs as me 'cause she goes to High School. Oh, I forgot to tell you; Loui is really Louise and she's my big sister. If I have a question that I don't want to ask Mum or Dad, she always helps me. But we don't really hang out together anymore. She's always going out to her friends' places.

Last night, Dad called us into the lounge room for our family prayer time. I think Mum must have been sick 'cause she looked really sad. Dad said they had been to the doctor for their regular baby check-up and that the news wasn't good. Loui and I looked at each other and I knew what she was thinking. She always looks out for me. I'm so lucky. It's almost as if I have two mums… but my second mum doesn't give me jobs.

'We may a problem with the baby,' Dad said. He was very serious. I could tell he was worried by how he sounded. 'The doctor said he might have something wrong with his heart.'

'Wait. Am I having a baby brother? That's cool. I asked Jesus to make it a baby brother and He's answered my prayer and…'

'That's what you got out of that? Seriously, Mim? Dad's telling us the family has a problem and you're rattling on again about you?' Loui spoke gently but she was serious, too.

Mum had to spend the next three months resting so that meant Loui and I would have more jobs to do. Everyone else was really praying hard for a healing miracle. I just asked for my new baby brother to come quickly so I could play with him.

Before school this morning, I had a chance to cuddle up to Mum on the lounge. I carried her a cup of tea after Loui made it for her and I sat down next to her. She drew me into her cuddle, like she always does, and we talked about the baby.

'Are you ok with the news about your little brother?' she asked softly.

'What do you mean, Mum?' I was a bit confused.

'Well,' she began, 'you may not be able to play with him as you thought. He may need special care for a while. He may even need special care for his whole life.'

'Well, take him to Dr Williamson. He'll fix him. He fixed my ears when they were sore.'

'It's not that simple, Mim,' Mum said. 'He's still in my tummy, growing, and we won't see him for a few more months, yet.'

You could have knocked me over with a feather! In her *tummy!* Was that why she was getting fat? I just thought she ate too many of her delicious biscuits, or something. I should have known 'cause she always told me not to have too many. 'Two is your limit,' she would always say. But then, how *could* I know? Nobody told me babies came from tummies.

That's weird. Surely that's not right.

'Mum?'

I just needed to check. Did she really know where babies came from? If she was right, how did he get in there? I mean. It doesn't make sense.

'How did my brother get in there?'

I wondered if she heard me 'cause she smiled, and then took a while before she answered. Finally she did.

'Do you remember the story of Miriam and Moses from the Bible?' She didn't really wait for me to answer. She just carried on. 'Moses needed help to stay alive and his own mother couldn't help him.'

I looked up at Mum and she had little tears creeping out of her eyes.

'She made him a special basket and, after praying to God, she put him in the basket and then hid him in the river. I don't think she expected his basket to drift off, but it did. That was her way of protecting him. So your little brother is in a kind of basket, too—my tummy. Do you understand?'

Understand? No way. This is getting so weird. But I nodded so that it would make her feel better.

'When you were in hospital, last year, that was kind of like your basket. You needed a place where you would be looked after, and protected, and Dr Williamson made sure you were ok. So, your little brother is in his basket so that he can be protected.'

'And that's when you got Button for me, to look after me when you weren't around. I love Button. He's kind of a goofy-looking rabbit, and a bit grungy 'cause we do all our jobs together. I tell him all my secrets (like how Mitch, at school, has a crush on me but I'm not interested), and like how I felt when I lost my first tooth, and…' (Mum was smiling). 'I'm running on again, aren't I? Sorry.'

It was time for Tiana and me to walk to school. I couldn't concentrate for thinking about my baby brother. What could *I* do to help protect him? If he was needing as much protection as Mum and Dad were saying, I had to do my part too. After all, I was his Mim. I would look after him the same way Miriam looked after her little brother, Moses. I knew what I had to do and couldn't wait to get home after school. But I had to wait a whole day.

'Mum. I can't find Button anywhere. Have you seen him?'

'I've been here all day, honey bunny. Isn't he on your bed where you normally put him?'

'No.' I couldn't help the tears from creeping into my eyes. It was really important to find him. Not just because he was my Button—I had a really important thing to ask him.

'Where did you last put him? Is he on your bookshelf? Did you look under your bed?

So many questions: *I don't know; no; yes.* 'He isn't anywhere.'

Mum was so understanding. I don't know how she does it but she always knows how I feel, and when I need a cuddle. I know I'm a big girl now, but I still need Mum-cuddles. 'Let's ask Jesus. Maybe He can help.'

She asks Jesus about everything. It works for her so I guess He might help me find Button. I'm not sure how He'll help but I'm ready to give it a go. Finding Button is important.

'Before we pray, let me ask you a question. Do you think that Jesus can help?'

Whoa, what? Me? I wanted to nod, even though I wasn't really sure, but somehow I sensed that the answer to this question was a bit more important than understanding how my little brother got into Mum's tummy.

Hesitantly I said, 'I'm not really sure. I think so.'

'That's ok, Mim. God tells us that He won't even snuff out a candle that's just smoking. That means that, even if our faith is so tiny, He won't expect any more from us than we can give. He'll accept even the tiniest bit of faith.'

'I think I'm ready to ask Jesus to help me find Button.'

So we began.

When I got into bed that night, my blankets were too tight and I had to pull them from between the wall and the bed.

'Dad! Guess what. I found Button.' I was so excited. Dad didn't know about my prayer with Mum so I told him all about it. That night, we added a special thank-you prayer to Jesus for helping me find Button. I don't know how he got there, but Jesus did, and He helped me find him. Button helped my faith to grow big, just like Mum's.

After Dad turned out the lights, Button and I had a serious conversation. I explained about our family's problem and he agreed with everything I said. I went to sleep knowing that we were doing the right thing.

'I've called Dr Williamson. He said to go straight to the hospital and he'll meet us there.' How could anyone sleep with Dad calling out in the hallway, just outside my bedroom. 'Loui is awake. She said she'd get Mim off to school in the morning.' I could tell something strange was happening so I crept into Loui's bedroom to see if she would tell me. All Dad said when he saw me out of bed was: 'Go back to sleep, Mim.' *As if I could!*

Loui told me Mum was having her baby. 'What do you mean, "having her baby"?'

'Boy, you don't know anything about babies, do you?' Loui said.

'I know Mum has a special basket to keep my little brother safe,' I said, proudly displaying my knowledge of babies. 'You know, like Moses.'

Loui nearly fell off the bed laughing. That wasn't the response I was expecting at all.

Ignoring her response, I asked when we would meet him. Loui said it probably wouldn't be for a few more days. The doctors would probably have to test him and make sure he was ok.

She was right. It took a whole three days before Dad took us both to the hospital to meet Joshua, my little brother. Mum was beaming from ear to ear. Dad led us all in a prayer of thanks, right there in the hospital. He explained that the doctors had done all sorts of tests on Joshua and couldn't find anything wrong with his heart. Dr Williamson just said it was God's blessing to us as a family.

As I cuddled up to Mum on the bed, I asked her if I could give Button to Joshua.

'But isn't he your special friend, Mim?'

'Well, he was, he is. No, he was, but I want Joshua to have him so Button can look after him like he looked after me. Button showed me that God doesn't mind if I have the tiniest amount of faith, as long as I do have faith.'

Seeing Mum's wrinkled forehead, I went on, 'Remember when he was lost? Button was showing me I just had to have faith in Jesus to find him. Maybe Button will help Joshua to have faith, too.'

Mum just pulled me in close and smiled.

Birmingham – Shop 43

TERRY GATFIELD

$\mathcal{I}$t was a frosty morning; coat collar to tingling ears, and woolly mittens. Close to my home, and on route to work, I walked past a row of smallish old shops nestled at the end of a dark, dank alleyway. Most of them were derelict and long since closed, with cheap, plywood sheets nailed across windows—a target for graffiti. I averted my eyes from the grotesque slogans and drawings of genitalia

This was Birmingham, eviscerated by the World War II, Luftwaffe and Thatcherite denationalisation policies—however, some smoke-black engineering factories remained, and the odd steam-factory whistle could still be heard. The canals, gasometers, craftsmen and artisans continued to survive the rampages of time. This city had been gutted of its soul, nevertheless I loved and enjoyed it, feeling proud to have called it 'home', albeit for a brief period.

But one of the shops remained defiant. It stayed un-boarded and emerged as if from the pages of a Dickensian novel.

The flaking paint over the shop's entrance introduced me to Jacobson and Sons. It had a number underneath which ended in '43 but time and the cold-damp Birmingham weather had eroded the history of the numeric. It could have been 1743, or 1843; but it may possibly have been just the raw street number. Outside hung the remains of a broken and defunct gas lamp, its life abruptly truncated by vandals.

On my morning walk to work each day, I peered into the small dark window of what I affectionately called 'Shop 43'. Squinting through the glass, I would visually encounter a bearded, timeworn craftsman with simple hand tools, stripping and rebuilding time-forgotten furniture. For fear of being caught out as a voyeur or accused of being an intruder, I would spend only a handful of seconds trying to unravel the mystery of the stories I had accumulated in my mind — stories that grew thicker and deeper over many months.

On this particular chilly winter morning, I was earlier than usual going to work and thus had time on my hands to indulge my inquisitiveness. It was difficult to see into the shop as no lights were on inside and I could only make out some faint shadowy hints created from the fading watts of the nearby streetlamp. I pushed my face firmly against the wavy pane of Victorian glass in the doorway, then suddenly froze. A large cold hand wrapped itself round the back of my neck. I gasped, as the ensuing adrenalin rushing to my reflexes spun me around.

It was the white-bearded craftsman piercing me with his dark brown eyes buried deep under bushy eyebrows. In a deep, rich Jewish accent, he said, reverently, 'Oh, I am sorry to startle you. My name is Isaac Jacobson. I have often seen you in the mornings looking into my workshop. You obviously have a great interest in my craft.' He paused briefly and continued, 'If you have time, you are most welcome to come in and see what I do.'

'I'd be delighted to,' I muttered. It was just as well I had left early for work that morning.

The timber-stained, rustic floors of his workshop had cavernous gaps, and the peeling paint on the walls was etched with age, as from a distant past. My nostrils flared with the pungent odour of resin, old books, and decaying leather. Isaac's dress was simple with an adorable animal skin apron sporting a bulging marsupial pouch, while his head was adorned with a black shtreimel, typically worn by Hasidic Jews. It gave him a learned and dignified appearance. I turned and caught sight of a sepia family portrait hanging on the wall of some seven or so people set in the dark ages at the turn of the last century—the patriarch and matriarch central to the narrative— replete with a menorah symbolically placed on a side table. He caught my gaze.

'I see you have just encountered my family. The Nazi regime was not kind to them and only I remain—the small child on the left is me.' He pointed with his gnarled timber-stained index finger. I felt awkward, and in the minute of silence I looked away.

Then I turned my eyes to the fabric of the workshop. The spirit of care, craftsmanship and passion oozed from every crack and crevice. This was no ordinary room but one created over aeons of time, richly embroidered with patience and love. Isaac took me verbally and visually on the journey of furniture restoration.

Whilst rubbing his palm over the top of an old timber table, Jacob said, 'The furniture cracks, grime and flaking shellac matter little—these can easily be rectified. But just as God looks at our hearts and sees the beauty there, I can be certain that beneath the furniture's surface imperfections my work will unveil fine oak, mahogany, walnut or cedar.'

He continued, 'First it is necessary to carefully strip the countless years of dirt, paint, and other accumulated materials from the surface. This has to be done gently but firmly with sharp scrapers so as to remove the top surface without damaging the timber beneath.'

Jacob's next comment took me by surprise. 'Occasionally, restoration may require the use of harsh chemicals, but this stage has to be managed with care. However, the witnesses of history have to remain in the fabric, even faint scars, small stains and scratches. Every item has its own story to tell. The furniture has to be embraced as history. It too has a soul.'

With a faraway look in his eyes, Jacob went on to recount, 'My father died at Auschwitz in my teen years—a devastating loss—but I was blessed with my fine Polish Uncle Levi who mentored me and gave me my passion for furniture restoration. He taught me the art of handling surface damages, corner injuries, or cracks that called out for repair. Sometimes furniture needed to be re-dowelled and glued to return it to its former strength and posture. Frequently, the timber has to be gently re-stained, for enhancement, calling for discernment and care.

'Uncle Levi taught me that once the natural beauty of the original timber had been restored, it needed sealing with shellac. Sometimes fifteen to twenty coats were necessary, followed each time by gentle caressing with soft wire wool. This operation was incomplete until every piece of the timber yielded its own original character. Finally, the surface had to be enriched with a natural beeswax polish, until it was possible to see deep down into the natural heart of the timber where the grain echoed its God-made dignity. The final goal was reached when the craftsman could see his or her own reflection in the timber, as if in a dark mirror.'

My all-too-brief apprenticeship with the master artist was a baptism of wonder into another world of time lost. As my visit came to its close, we said our goodbyes after sharing a warm hug.

Snow was gently falling as I left the workshop and ventured out into the cold morning. The shrill call of a local factory whistle pierced the air with a jet of hot steam remaining in its wake. I turned up the collar of my long coat and started to think long and hard about my own life.

On reflection, it occurred to me that my life was like a mirror of the craftsman's skill that I experienced that morning. I, too, was in the process of being restored to a place of beauty and loveliness. Yet, mine was not an outward expression but an inner journey—a journey of the soul. This was the handiwork and craftsmanship of God. Life for me had been somewhat brutal and damaging—damage caused by changing circumstances, by others and through my own wilfulness and foolishness—many things of regret! Through surrender, prayer and support of friends, I was able to see the silent hand and heart of God enacted in repair and restoration of my life to a place of healing and increasing wholeness. Perhaps that process continues with me to this day—restoration I find to be a slow yet deep process.

I left Birmingham shortly after my experience with the master craftsman and did not reconnect with the city for a decade or so. On my last visit, I found Birmingham had become gentrified, and alas 'Shop 43,' along with all the others in that dark alleyway, had disappeared, replaced by sterile high-rise apartments. However, the refreshing life-changing, catalytic memory of that encounter will stay with me for the remainder of my life.

A Lifetime of Memories

KAREN ROPER

As was my usual habit on a Saturday, I went to my grandmother's house to check on her and have afternoon tea. It wasn't that she needed checking on too much as she was still quite agile, and her memory was still sharp. These afternoons were for me—I cherished her company and her shared wisdom that often came through stories of long ago. Although I am sure she looked forward to our afternoons together too.

Walking up her front doorstep, I stopped to admire the flowers in her garden. Her motto was: *flowers in the front garden and vegetables in the back garden.* She never wavered from this as long as I had known her.

Rapping on the front door, I could hear her loudly say, 'Come in.' I opened the front door, which was already unlocked, and started to wander in. 'I am in the formal dining room,' I heard her say.

Walking up the hallway, with photos on either side, I turned a corner and made my way to the formal dining room. I just started to walk into the room when I came to an abrupt halt. Here was grandma sitting at the table, with a big photo frame in front of her and all these pieces of glass were sitting around her.

Did she break something? I wondered. No, on closer inspection as I resumed walking to the table, they were all bits of coloured glass.

'Grandma!' I exclaimed, 'What are you doing?'

'Hi there, you look pretty today,' she retorted, not really answering my question.

I noticed that the glass on the big photo frame was sitting against the far wall and that on the backing of the frame were stuck photos of my grandma at various stages of her life. There was a baby photo, a toddler photo, a primary school photo, a high school photo and what looked like one photo from each decade of her life from her twenties to her seventies. But what was she doing with those coloured pieces of glass?

Grandma finally answered my question, 'I am reflecting on my life and making a picture of it. I wanted to surprise you once it was finished. Why are you here so early?'

'I am not early but right on time,' I said.

'Really, then time must have got away from me,' Grandma stated with a puzzled look on her face. 'Let's have some tea. I think I forgot to have lunch.'

She rose from her chair and led the way into the kitchen to make the cup of tea and find some goodies to go with it, from her baking that she had done that week. I started to ask her about the picture frame, but she gave me a look that stated that topic was off-bounds.

The rest of the afternoon's visit went surprisingly well as we enquired about each other's week and shared funny stories and anecdotes from the past.

As I left her house that day, I couldn't help but wonder what that picture frame meant and why all that coloured glass.

The next few weeks past uneventfully. I still went to Grandma's for afternoon tea on Saturdays, but noticed that the dining room door was shut each time I went there. If she thought I was going to forget about that picture frame, well, that was not happening.

Finally, about eight weeks later, Grandma greeted me at the front door as I arrived at her house. It was clear that she had been waiting for me to come.

'Hello,' I said, 'what a nice surprise,' as she opened the door even before I had a chance to knock.

There was an air of excitement around her. 'Come with me,' she exclaimed. I followed her, eager with anticipation, up the hallway, past those family photos and around the corner. The dining room door was finally open. As she led me over to the dining table, I couldn't help but feel a little bit of trepidation overlay my excitement as I came closer to the table.

There laid out on the table was the most beautiful picture I had seen. Those little bits of coloured glass surrounded each of the photos that I had seen previously. It was truly a masterpiece.

'Let me explain the picture to you.' Grandma picked up a piece of cloth from the sideboard. She covered the picture frame with it and only exposed the first photo and the glass around it.

It was not as spectacular as the whole but didn't look too bad.

Grandma pointed to the photo. 'I wanted to do a picture frame setting out my life story. I chose different photos of me from my childhood all the way up to the present day. But I didn't know how I was going to explain the things that had happened to me. It would take too long to write, so I prayed about it. God told me to use the coloured glass. So, I chose red, blue, green and yellow glass.

'The red glass is for those painful times in my life. The green glass was for the good times. The blue glass was when I did things my own way and didn't seek God and the yellow glass was when I felt closest to God.'

She paused before going on:

'The baby photo has mostly green glass around it as I don't really remember my baby years, but I know they must have been good.'

She uncovered the next photo:

'The toddler photo has mostly green but a little red, as my grandma passed away at the time. She made me feel really special and I can still remember the chocolate chip cookies she made for me.'

Then she uncovered the next photo:

'My primary school years have some green glass but mostly red and a little blue, as I was abused at this time by a family friend. There were some good times like going away on a beach holiday and some blue as I tried to hide my pain on my own.'

Tears were streaming down both of our faces as she shared the story of her primary school years. Maybe that was enough for one day—I would be there the next weekend, when she could uncover more. 'Grandma, this is too painful. Let's have tea now and we will uncover the others next week.'

Grandma agreed and we went to have tea.

All that week, I reflected on what she had told me and wondered whether the story was about to get better or worse. As I arrived at her house the following Saturday, it was with more trepidation than excitement at what this weekend would bring.

As she let me in, we walked into the dining room, both lost in thought.

Grandma uncovered the next photo of her high school years. I could see that this one finally had some yellow around it.

Grandma explained, 'My high school years were good. I had lots of friends, the abuse had stopped and in tenth grade, I gave my life to Jesus.' The coloured glass was a mixture of green, blue and yellow around this photo.

She then uncovered the photo of her twenties. I knew some of this story, but I was surprised to see the coloured glass around this photo had no yellow.

Grandma sighed. 'My twenties were my hardest years. I walked away from God, met your grandfather and gave birth to your mother. I told you that granddad died but he didn't, he just left us. I still have no idea where he is. That is why there is a mixture of green, red and blue. I thought my own way was best.'

The next photo was of her thirties and, for the first time, there was no red.

Excitement had come back into her voice. 'My thirties were glorious; I had my little girl and had secured employment. My parents used to babysit her, and I eventually saved up enough money to buy this house. But something more exciting happened, I invited Jesus back into my life. My life had purpose again.'

She uncovered the next photo of her forties, and it was similar to her thirties but there was even more yellow. 'My life continued on the same but my relationship with Jesus grew stronger.'

I started to catch her excitement, and I was glad she had created this picture frame. Earlier on, I wasn't so sure as it had brought up painful memories for her and had uncovered them for me. The cloth moved a bit further down the picture frame. I noticed that this photo had red again. 'My fifties were a time of loss and sorrow for me. My parents died in my fifties and my girl left home. I felt like I was all alone in my house for the first time, but I wasn't really alone as Jesus was here.'

She moved the cloth down a little bit further. Red was again missing from this photo, and I noticed blue had not been around the photos for a number of years. 'My sixties were another decade of good times. You were born and that made my life worth living again. I retired from work and have been able to travel and do all the things I always wanted to do. Jesus was still with me and always will be.'

At last, she moved the cloth off the entire picture frame but just as quickly, she covered up everything but the seventies photo. I noticed that this photo had all yellow. 'My seventies are a time when I realised that my life was only worth living if I was living it for Jesus fully. So ministry work has taken up a lot of my time. Even our afternoon teas are ministry work as I disciple and love on you, so you don't make the same mistakes I have.'

As she took the cloth off, I looked at the photo as a whole and realised our lives are made of good times, bad times, times before we met Jesus and times after we met Jesus.

But just like the picture frame, our lives come together in one mosaic to tell the story of God's grace and mercy in our lives for others to see and experience.

As grandma and I walked out of the dining room and went to the kitchen to make tea, I told her my reflections. She looked at me, smiled, and said the picture frame was worth it all just to hear me say that.

All of our lives are like that picture frame but, if God is at the centre of our lives, He crafts them to make each of our experiences add up to make the total stories individually of each of our lives.

Helga's Decision

LINDA SHIELDS

Helga had been a children's nurse for seven years and loved working at the home for disabled children on the outskirts of Berlin. Her family were devout Catholics, with a strong belief that all life was sacred.

Her poor father had spent six months in the concentration camp at Dachau for 're-education' and, although his health was damaged, he had steadfastly, albeit secretly, held onto his Catholic beliefs. He was horrified when Helga told him that, to obtain her job, she had to swear an oath of obedience to the German Chancellor and Führer, Adolf Hitler. This was a mandatory requirement for all nurses working in Germany at the time, and so she had no choice if she wanted to keep working in her profession.

War was looming in Europe when, in 1939, Hitler ordered that all disabled children's institutions in Germany and Austria were to begin a new programme. The purpose of this project was to save the suffering of children, and so relieve the burden they placed on the German community. Helga was confused about what this meant.

Two years later, in 1941, a directive came from the senior nurse, Schwester Lotte, that the new initiative was to be implemented. The Nazis were strong, direct, and uncompromising. Their race laws discriminated against minority groups, most particularly Jews, but also those who were considered 'useless eaters' and a burden on the nation—disabled and chronically ill people. Some members of the community thought such laws were right, important and necessary for the common good of the whole country. Many people were worried by the laws, but because speaking

---

Nazi racial laws were implemented across Germany, Austria and Occupied Europe. As well as Jews, other racial and religious groups, those deemed 'sub-human', and people with chronic conditions such as disabilities, epilepsy, alcoholism, mental illness and incurable diseases were deemed unfit for life, or a burden on the Nazi State. They were killed. These murders took place in hospitals and institutions for disabled and chronically ill people, and in psychiatric hospitals. The killing programme had its own government department and was known as the 'T4' programme, after the address of the house in Berlin which was its headquarters. Exact numbers of people killed are unknown, but it is estimated that at least 10,000 children, mostly German and Austrian citizens, and well over 100,000 adults were murdered (https:// encyclopedia.ushmm.org/content/en/article/euthanasia-program). Doctors signed the documents which certified that a person was to be killed, but it was mainly nurses who did the killing. After the war, many doctors were tried for their roles in T4, but very few nurses were ever indicted or indeed punished. (Benedict S and Shields L (eds), *Nursing and Midwifery in Nazi Germany: the 'euthanasia programs'*, Routledge History: London, 2014).

out against them could lead to prison—or worse—few were brave enough to speak openly.

Helga was troubled. She lost her appetite and tossed and turned all one night trying to make sense of the new ideas the Nazis were imposing across all of German society. Along with some of her friends, she had been to see the latest film *Ich klage an* ('I Accuse'), starring one of Helga's favourite actors, Paul Hartmann. In it, the doctor husband of a young woman suffering from multiple sclerosis, arranged for her to be 'put out of her misery'. He was hailed as a hero for making the hard decision to have his wife killed, thus fulfilling the dream of the Third Reich—to eliminate anyone who was a burden on the state. The term often used was a 'life unworthy of life'.

Recently, schoolchildren had been visiting the children's home to look at their disabled peers, to see that they were 'useless feeders' and had 'lives not worth living'. Helga could not understand how killing disabled and sick people just because they were considered a burden on the country could be right. She discussed this with her friends over lunch.

'Oh!' said Gertrud. 'The Führer has said that the Reich will never be strong unless people like this don't exist.'

'If the Führer said it, it must be right,' said Berte.

'But,' said Helga, 'we are nurses, and we must care for people no matter who they are.'

The other girls started to look uneasy. One said, 'Helga, keep your voice down. If Schwester Lotte hears you talking like that, she'll report you to the Party. Who knows what might happen then?'

Helga finished her lunch and went back to work.

A few weeks later, Schwester Lotte called the nurses together and told them that a specialist carer, Nurse Gretel, was coming from Hadamar, a large hospital for people with mental illnesses and disabilities. 'Nurse Gretel is trained in compassionate ways to end a life,' she said.

'Does this mean that she will be ending the lives of some of our children?' asked Helga.

Schwester Lotte replied sternly, 'We must keep this quiet. Please do not talk about it amongst your families. There will be procedures put in place to make sure it all flows smoothly. I expect you all to remember your oath of obedience to the Führer, co-operate with Nurse Gretel, and show her consideration. After all, it is a very difficult job that she's doing.'

The next day, Helga was working on the ward where her favourite little boy, Ernst, lived. Ernst had cerebral palsy and had spent most of his life at the home. His parents had been told that, if they did not let Ernst go to the institution, they would lose their jobs. So they had little choice. However, they were told that Ernst would have a good life and be cared for with compassion and kindness.

Georg, Helga's senior nurse, asked that she get Ernst ready to meet Nurse Gretel the following week.

'Does this mean that he will be killed?' she asked.

'Not necessarily,' said Georg, 'but we must have him ready for assessment.' Seeing a Nazi Party pin in Georg's collar, Helga decided not to say anything.

That night, however, she discussed her fears with her father. 'What should I do?' Helga asked in tears.

Her father had suffered at the hands of the Nazis and knew firsthand how severe punishment could be for those who disagreed with orders.

Helga picked at her food. 'After all, I did swear an oath of allegiance to Hitler, and Hitler himself has decreed that all disabled children must be killed.'

Her father, a wise and kindly man, was greatly troubled by seeing his beloved daughter in such a dilemma. 'Well,' he said, 'there are several things you could do. You could do exactly what you are being ordered to do. You would be fulfilling your oath of obedience and, in the future, when you think about it, you will be able to say, "I was just following orders." After all, Hitler won't last forever, and one day you may be held accountable for your role. Or, you could leave and find another job somewhere else, perhaps in a hospital or clinic where people are being cured rather than killed, perhaps a military hospital with wounded soldiers. You would be helping the State and not be putting yourself in a situation where you have to make difficult choices. Though…' He paused. '…this may not help your conscience when it comes to Ernst and the other children.'

Helga considered her father's advice.

He continued: 'The most difficult thing to do would be to try and find a way to stop Ernst and other children from having assessments, or meeting Nurse Gretel. Is there a way to have Ernst moved to another hospital? Or perhaps contact his parents to ask them to take him home?'

'Oh no,' said Helga, 'I'm much too junior to be able to do any of those things.'

'Then there's one more solution that might be possible—though you would need my help, and the help of others in the village. Could you, perhaps with the help of another nurse, smuggle Ernst out of the home and we can hide him until this blasted regime is over? After all, there are people in this village and the next town who are hiding Jewish children. Perhaps we could hide Ernst as well. Remember, Helga, there is danger in all these solutions. You, and whoever helps you, could end up in a concentration camp. Opposition to the Nazis is being stamped out all over Germany and Austria. If you are caught trying to help or hide Ernst, they will take a very dim view of that. You could be executed. But also remember that you and your conscience have to live for the rest of your life with whatever decision you make. I can't help you with that.'

Helga's father looked her directly in the eyes. 'You must decide for yourself.'

Emma

JENNY WOOLSEY

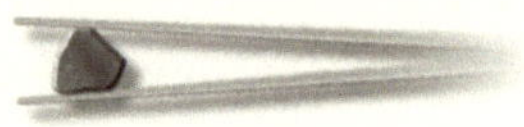

*C*rash!

Emma screamed and jumped, dodging the ceramic shards flying like heat-seeking missiles at her legs. Tears welled in her eyes.

On the polished wooden floor, the precious heirloom lay shattered … just like her life. 'Oh no! Grandma, I'm so sorry.'

Meow. Harold jumped off the display cabinet, landing with a thud on the floor at her feet.

'Harold, why did you do that?' She hid her face with her hands, and wept.

Sweat dripped down Emma's forehead and her T-shirt stuck to her back.

The kettle clicked off with a tired sigh. She poured the hot water over a tea bag that had already done two rounds that week. She dunked it until the water turned a light brown … and kept dunking, aiming to strengthen her drink.

Emma opened the window above the sink, hoping for a breeze. There wasn't one. She could switch on the pedestal fan but that would add to the electricity bill. The last one was overdue. How long before they'd disconnect her?

Her stomach growled like a garbage disposal and she opened the fridge. Inside, as she knew, were two carrots, a half empty longlife milk carton, a few slices of bread and a tub of margarine. In the cupboard was a bag of cat food, a couple of noodle cups, a tin of spaghetti, a small vegemite jar, a few tea bags and half a packet of rice crackers.

Harold rubbed his face on her legs. She reached down and patted his soft fur. 'What am I going to do?'

She spread a miniscule amount of margarine and vegemite on her bread, then took her tea and lunch to the table. Listless, she reached to open her mail.

'Second overdue notice electricity account. Overdue water account. Termination of Lease—Two weeks to vacate.'

She turned each piece of paper face down and ran her fingers through her hair. Harold jumped up onto the table. 'Harold, it looks like we're going to be homeless.' Tears wet the bills.

Emma's battered Corolla was parked under the blooming jacaranda. Delicate purple flowers lay scattered across its roof. She packed her two suitcases, a few garbage bags full of odds and ends as well as Harold's litter box into the boot and on the back seat, leaving room for the cat carrier. She had done her best at cleaning the unit. If it wasn't up to scratch she'd lose her bond but she couldn't do anything about that either. Harold yowled.

'Yeah, I don't like this either.' She pushed her key into the ignition and the motor grunted to life. Toni Child's lament blared from the CD player.

Leaving Mitchelton behind, she made her way to Redcliffe. She didn't know what to do once she got there.

At Sutton's Beach the waves flowed in and back out. Emma sat, hunched over. She'd been at her job for two years, earning good money while living with Grandma. They'd travelled overseas, gone out on the town each weekend and had fun. At the time she didn't think she needed to save.

'Em, can you please come to my office?' Grant had said to her at work, as she photocopied some paperwork.

'Sure. I'll be there in a minute.' She finished her task then ventured to Grant's office. She sat opposite him and stared at the photo of his smiling family. Her heart ached for Grandma … six hollow months since her fatal heart attack.

Grant cleared his throat. 'The firm is making cutbacks and I have to let some people go. I'm sorry, Emma, but you're one of them. I am giving you two weeks' notice.'

It took a minute to process the words. 'Oh,' was all she could manage. 'Two weeks?'

'Yes. I'll write you a good reference. I'm sorry.'

Grant's eyebrows furrowed. He looked genuine.

She applied for numerous jobs … but heard nothing back. It seemed no one wanted her skillset. Then she tried for jobs that didn't require any particular skills. She lasted just two weeks in a call centre—fired for not attaining the daily quota of sales. She tried a coffee shop but they said she was too slow. Her meagre savings disappeared quickly. She'd been able to rent on her own, after all it was a one-bed unit, and had contacted her landlord. He seemed okay about her situation.

Each week though, even on unemployment benefits, she slipped behind. And finally, after missing two months' rent, her landlord said she had to go.

Emma drove the car to the shopping centre in Kippa Ring, parking between two trucks. Harold lay on her lap. She patted him. He purred.

'This is where we… we're sleep… sleeping.' The words caught in her throat and sobs escaped her lips. 'What is going to happen to us?'

Emma reclined the seat as far as she could and shoved her pillow up against the window. She hugged Harold then closed her eyes. 'Look out for the boogie man.'

She tried to sleep but every little noise woke her. By morning her nerves were fried.

Days blurred. Over time Emma worked out the best places to park overnight without being moved on—industrial estates, quiet corners of parks, carparks after dark.

She kept a pocket knife tucked under her seat. And whenever someone approached her car, she would grab it, her fingers trembling as she held it next to the door handle.

She began to sleep during the day. That was safer. Any noise at night startled her. Her nerves were brittle, her hair tousled and oily, and her face pale with bags under her eyes. She stared into her reflection, in the mirror, at the public pool where she showered once a week. This wasn't the Emma she knew.

'Grandma, I miss you so much!' she whispered. 'Why is this happening to me?'

With hope diminishing, Emma aimlessly drove around. The world outside her windscreen now seemed to belong to someone else—people rushing to go to work, parents pushing prams, little kids scooting to school, cafés buzzing with laughter.

How was she going to get her life back on track? Would she die out here?

Taped on a thrift shop window in Scarborough, a sign advertised 'Free lunch and groceries, Thursdays' at a nearby church.

Today was Wednesday.

Desperate for food, she decided to go.

Emma slowly slid the church office door open. She held the cat carrier in her left hand.

A receptionist smiled at her. 'How can I help you?'

'Um, I'm here for the lunch and some groceries.' Emma stared at her dirty feet. 'I hope it's okay to bring my cat in.'

'Oh, he's so cute. What's his name? Come this way. My name's Amy. Have you been here before?' She talked very fast.

'His name is Harold. Ah, no.'

'Well, you are most welcome. I will take you out to Sarah who'll look after you.'

Emma felt the warmth in Amy's tone as they left through a back door, descended some steps and made their way to a hall.

Inside, Emma surveyed the many trestle tables set with white tablecloths, cutlery and glasses. Jugs of water and little bud vases with pink roses sat in the centre of each one. At the far end, on a long counter, were six slow cookers and platters of sliced French loaves and fruit. Her stomach ached as she inhaled the aromatic smells of brewed coffee, pumpkin soup and beef stew. She longed for a proper meal after eating tinned spaghetti and baked beans. Cold.

Three people had arrived: an elderly man with a long grey beard, a teenager holding a newborn and a guy about her age wearing a striped shirt.

Amy introduced her.

'Hello, Amy, welcome, I'm Sarah.' The lady smiled. Her blonde hair curled around her face. 'What's your cat's name?'

After some small talk—she wasn't going to give much away—Sarah led her to the empty chair beside Simon, the guy in the striped shirt.

'So, what brings you here?' Simon asked.

'Just passing through. How about you?'

'I've just lost my job and I'm looking for another.' He shrugged.

'I lost my job too. What did you do?'

The conversation continued until the hall was full of scraping chairs and chattering. A voice came over the microphone thanking everyone for coming.

'If you feel comfortable, please bow your head and we'll say grace.' Sarah, on the mic, closed her eyes. 'Thank You, Lord, for this food. Bless it to our bodies and strengthen us to face each day that lies before us. Amen.'

Emma had never been to church but she closed her eyes and followed along.

The beef stew tasted as good as it smelt, and she went back for seconds. She sopped up the rich brown gravy with the fresh bread.

Upon leaving, Sarah stopped her. 'Emma, I was wondering if you need somewhere to live?'

Emma paused. 'Ar, yes, actually. I've been living out of my car.'

'I thought so. We have some beds here for women and children if you would like to stay. We can also help you get back on your feet.'

'Oh, um, I'm not sure.' Emma didn't know why she baulked at it.

'We can help you access the services you need, and you'll be safe here.'

Tears filled Emma's eyes and dribbled down her cheeks.

Sarah touched her arm. 'And I'm sure everyone would love to have Harold around.'

That night, for the first time in weeks, Emma slept in a bed, with fresh sheets, snuggled in a cotton blanket. The air con was on and her neck lay straight. Harold curled up on her stomach.

She woke to the heavy pitter patter of raindrops on the Colourbond roof and cried into her pillow. Tears not of hopelessness but of hope.

Over the next few days, Angela and Margie from the church helped her to restart her life. She filled out application forms for public housing and job programs. She learnt to budget and how to look after her mental health.

The system moved slowly but with the help of the church, Emma could see a way forward.

Sarah brought in cat litter, food and treats for Harold. 'He's just so cute. I always wanted a cat but my husband's allergic to them.'

'Well, you can pat him as much as he'll let you.'

Sarah laughed. 'They say that about cats. Also, I've just found out there's an admin assistant position open at the camping store down the road. Would that interest you?'

Emma nodded. 'That would be great!'

'Awesome. I'll make a time for your interview.'

The next morning Emma met with Jane, the owner of the store. Afterwards, she tried to keep a straight face as she told Sarah, 'I got the job.'

Sarah clapped her hands. 'Congratulations! Thank You, Lord.'

Six months later, Emma stood in the doorway of a two-bedroom unit, managed by community housing. The walls were bare, the carpet thin—but it was hers.

Harold prowled the room, tail high, inspecting every corner. When he finally settled on the windowsill, purring in the sunlight, Emma smiled. She placed Grandma's photo on the table and whispered, 'We made it.'

On the weekend Sarah arrived with a kettle and toaster, a box of flavoured teas and a small plant in a mosaic pot. 'I made that pot myself,' she said.

'It's gorgeous.'

Emma placed the pot beside the photo. It was a great replacement for the one that broke.

'Who is that?' Sarah asked

'She is the greatest lady I have ever known—my grandmother. Would you like a tea?'

Sarah nodded. 'Yes, please. I'd love to know more about her.'

Shattered

JUDY ROGERS

It's the seventeenth sun since our capture, and I'm shattered.
A mound of rocks rises in front of me.
A line of slaves stagger behind me.
A lifetime of bondage looms ahead of me.
Our captors jeer and taunt in words we don't understand.
Their grunting orders terrorise our every breath.
Giant red breastplates, ugly flat-topped heads, sparse scraggly oily hair, pointed teeth—heavy bludgeons.
We may not understand their guttural language, but we understand their bludgeons.
I stagger forward: thirsty, hungry, exhausted.
Thoughts of the years of slavery looming ahead engulf me in a dark tunnel of despair.
A whip cracks—close—too close.
Like a line of ants, we move, picking up rocks to transport up the hill—some need only one set of hands, some two, some more.

I swallow a smile at the memory of gathering wood in the forest, when our life was free.

We'd heard rumours of marauders—giant men from over the waters, but they were only rumours—whispers from travelling tinkers.

Our village was so distant from the sea, we thought we were safe.

I'd watched a line of ants that day—the day in the forest—a hundred lifetimes ago.

How persistent they were! How determined to carry away their prize crumbs.

Some needing one ant, some two, some more.

Now, we are the ants.

The rocks are our crumbs—there are no prizes.

Instead of the busyness of ants, there's only the shuffling of a mish-mash of broken male humanity, bullied by cruel, ugly, arrogant invaders.

They had descended onto our villages early one morning—

a blur of war-cries, whinnying horses, whips and screams, red faces, red uniforms—

red blood,

dragging away every able-bodied male, killing our cattle, and laughing at our women and children and elderly standing amongst our burning homes with nothing but tears and despair.

I will defeat them! I will find a way!

Determination spurs me on, but at sunset, I fall onto my rag bed on the hard rocky ground, with a bowl of thin stew and shattered dreams.

Jeers and whips lurch us out of the little slumber we have had.
Bread and water are supposed to revive us.
Day eighteen begins, the same way as the last seventeen.
More rocks, more whips, more jeers,
More ugly flat-heads, another bowl of sad stew and day eighteen finishes
the same way as the last seventeen.
But something feels different.
Nothing looks different—but I can feel something in the air.
I glance around, searching amongst the broken, grime-laden men for my fellow villagers
—for my friends—those I've known all my life.
All around me, shoulders stoop—many too young to be carrying such loads
and many too old.
Speaking is forbidden, but I can hear every heartbeat,
every sadness,
every despair,
every heartache and every pain.
What is happening to me?
Someone creeps close. I can feel his breath in my ear. 'Be prepared. It's coming.'
I turn, but I'm alone. Shattered in body and spirit and now hearing voices.
Day nineteen begins.
Day nineteen ends.
Day twenty begins.
Jeers, whips, hard bread, water, endless rocks.

I can hardly contain the feeling of anticipation. Something is going to happen.

Tonight, a different set of soldiers guards us.

Their faces are hidden, their quietness unnerving. Tonight, there is no jeering, no bludgeons, no whips.

Tonight, our stew is hot and thick.

Disbelief is overcome by hunger, distrust by deprived tastebuds.

When I reach for my bowl, my hand tingles.

I risk an upward glance at the man serving.

His eyes are blue. His gaze clear.

He holds my hand firm, looks into my eyes and whispers, 'Lead the men. Climb the rocks. Do not delay. No matter what happens.'

The same voice! The one I thought I'd dreamed.

He releases my bowl and turns to the next man. I stand dumbfounded until I'm pushed along the line.

Day twenty-one begins with hard bread and water—

And rain.

Beautiful, refreshing, cool, cleansing rain.

Relentless rain.

By mid-morning rivulets cover our ankles. We slog our rocks through the mud.

Clouds hide the sun.

Time is impossible to tell.

The water rises, tumbling and rushing, knocking some men over.

Then it happens.

A roar like a dragon's screech pierces the air.

The side of the cliff behind us crumbles in a tumult of mud
and trees and rocks and boulders.
Our captors stumble down the hill—abandoning us to the
dragon's vengeance—
Their red breastplates muddied, their whips dragging,
their bludgeons abandoned.
It's time! I know it.
'Climb the rocks!' I yell.
Some heed me. Some don't.
'To the rocks! To the rocks!' Others take up my urging.
Some heed us. Some don't.
Those who delay are swept away in the dragon's maw of
destruction.
More and more men, bedraggled, wheezing, shivering,
panicking,
swarm up the pile of rocks, once their certain death, now
their salvation.
Night falls with a chill and a sky filled with stars calling to
be plucked.
How many men followed me up the rock pile I have no idea.
My heart aches for those who didn't.
I'm even sad for the enemy. For those who mocked us and
destroyed our lives.
I wonder how many of them were conscripted into the regime
of terror they were part of.
How many more mothers and fathers will now grieve
because a greedy man in a distant kingdom craved power
and dominion?

Dawn gouges the sky with slashes of red and orange.
We stand, gaping at the landscape below.
The land is empty—clear of any sign of our invaders.
Not a man, not a horse, not a wagon, not a tent.
All has been tumbled away with the wrath of the dragon's rain.
We're alone.
A mosaic of shattered rain-streaked men, muddy and thankful, saved by the whisper of a stranger.
A lone singer raises his voice—it's him!
'Who are you?' I whisper.
He looks at me, smiles and nods and fades into the mist.
Others have taken up the stirring melody.
More join in—then more and more.
Hope and determination join with courage, resolve and confidence, collecting pieces of our shattered selves and glueing the fragments together.
We are victorious.
Forever grateful to the warning of salvation in a whisper of grace.

Unprepared

INGRID DACKER

Red dust spiralled upward, kicked along by the restless movement of horses' hooves. Twitching legs and swirling tails did not deter the ever-present, annoying flies. The horses sought refuge from the blazing sun in the shade of an old gum tree but it did little to bring relief from the searing heat. The unrelenting drought had laid waste the landscape.

Even the old farmhouse looked defeated, drooping sadly, with only the chimney holding its own against the ravages of time and gravity. Its greying walls, swathed in red dust, had long since lost the last hint of paint.

Two young blue heelers gave us an enthusiastic welcome before they retreated to the shade of the crooked old tank stand. My husband James and I had come to visit our friend Tom in Central New South Wales. Not unexpectedly, there was no answer to our knocking so we headed towards the horse yards. We found Tom checking on his horses. We leaned on the fence as his stallion nuzzled his hands looking for a treat. In his prime, this beautiful, fiery animal had been meant to turn Tom's fortunes around but nothing had happened as he had hoped. The drought was wide spread and people were not parting with their money. He stared off into the distant heat haze as we made small talk about the weather and the rains that had eluded him.

As we walked towards the house we noticed that the gutters were twisted and dilapidated and in places not even connected to the old corrugated iron water tanks.

'How about I give you a hand to hang your gutters back up?' James asked. 'You know me. I don't like just sitting around. It's not much but it'd be a bit of a help. It's got to rain sometime.'

'No, don't bother. I've got too many other things to do. The whole lot needs replacing, just like everything else around here. But there is no way I can afford that. It doesn't matter. It hasn't rained in years and it's not going to start now. There's nothing predicted anytime soon.' Tom's voice held a hard edge.

James pressed him a bit more but Tom would have none of it. They had been mates for years and they had often worked on projects together—but not this time.

It was after we had eaten lunch together that Tom began to pour out his woes to us. The never-ending drought, the cost of feed for the few remaining animals, the empty dams and water tanks, the bank baying at his heels, the daily fight to stay afloat, it all came tumbling out. His wife had left, moving the children into the small town nearby. She had found employment and a new life without him. It was the last straw.

His wife had tried so hard to keep her little garden alive, faithfully reusing every bit of water. There was nothing to show for it now. She had also worked hard to keep their marriage alive. She still held hope for their family, their marriage, but Tom fed on a diet of anger and resentment that was slowly killing her resolve. He was angry with her, with his farm, with himself—but mainly with God. He felt that God had let him down, that the promises He had made had been broken. We are 'townies' and have no experience in the grinding, soul-destroying fight a farmer faces every day to survive under those conditions. We felt his pain, we listened, not saying much, just letting him vent his hopelessness and despair.

'Would you mind if we prayed for rain?' I ventured to ask unsure of how he would respond.

'I've tried that… doesn't work.'

'Could we try again? We have nothing to lose.'

'If you want.' Tom's voice held no enthusiasm and he kept his eyes on his work worn hands.

I decided to take him at his word.

The prayer was simple, a request to our loving Father for rain, for respite from the unrelenting drought. We knew that God understood and cared in a way that we could not.

It was about an hour later that we heard the crack of thunder. The sky became black and threatening as the storm headed in our direction.

'That doesn't mean a thing,' Tom brushed it off. 'Those storms blow up often but they just go right around without giving us anything.'

He was wrong. The rain came, heavy fat drops of sweet-smelling rain that increased until it was bucketing down.

Tom was suddenly galvanised into action. Together James and Tom struggled to prop up the sagging gutters while water cascaded in a torrent over the sides. Tom ran around like a dripping wet demented man trying to salvage at least some of the downpour. Very little made its way into the tired old tanks and what did erupted through the sizeable holes that mocked at Tom's attempts to stem the flow. There was one tank in reasonable condition that had retained a little. It would give a reprieve for a short time.

The dogs danced in circles revelling in the mud completely unaware of their master's plight.

The rain stopped as suddenly as it had begun. Muddy rivulets ran across the barren paddocks, snaking their way towards the empty dams. It was not enough to break the drought but it was something.

Did the water soak into the cracked hard ground to refresh and support new growth or was the ground so resistant that it just ran off? We didn't know.

It was heartbreaking and there was not a thing we could have done to change the outcome. God had answered our prayer but so much of the gracious gift had been wasted.

Our hope was that Tom's heart, so hardened by despair and disappointment, would soften again to receive the love that God longed to shower on him. The God for whom nothing is too difficult hadn't given up on him. His grace is still more than enough, always more than enough.

The Church of the Listening Christ

HAZEL BARKER

The old church on the hill had no congregation, no priest, and no roof. Only the wind attended its sermons now, rustling through the eucalyptus and whispering secrets to the stained glass that still clung stubbornly to its stone bones.

Maria found it by accident, or so she thought. She'd come to the town of Wattleford chasing a name—her grandmother's, etched into a forgotten immigration ledger from 1947. The locals spoke of her as if she were myth.

An old man said, 'Ah, yes, Linda used to walk barefoot through the frost and never caught cold.'

The church was where Linda had once prayed. The floor was a mosaic of shattered glass and moss. Maria stepped carefully, her boots crunching over fragments of saints and stars. At the altar, a single pane remained intact—a depiction of a woman cloaked in blue, hands outstretched.

Maria knelt. She didn't know why. She wasn't religious. But something in the air—thick with memory—pressed her gently, like a hand on her shoulder. 'I don't know what I believe,' she whispered.

The wind answered, curling around her like a baby's breath. And then, faintly, a voice—not spoken but felt. *You just have to remember.*

Maria closed her eyes. Images flickered behind her lids: a woman stirring soup with herbs she couldn't name, singing lullabies in a language she'd never learned, pressing a cool hand to a fevered brow. Her grandmother, Linda.

When she opened her eyes, the mosaic had changed. The glass shimmered, rearranged. The woman in blue now held a sprig of wattle in one hand, and in the other—a key.

Maria's heart thudded. She didn't understand it all. But she felt it. The faith that lives in memory. In blood. In the quiet places where stories wait to be told.

Outside, the wind carried her name down the hill to Jack the Widower. He lived in a weatherboard house near the creek, where the jacarandas bloomed too early and the mailbox leaned like it had given up.

Every morning, Jack sat on his porch with two cups of tea— one untouched, growing cold beside the empty chair. His wife, Ruth, had died three years ago. Stroke, sudden. She'd been hanging laundry when it happened.

Jack found her with a peg still clutched in her hand.

Since then, he'd stopped going to church. Stopped talking to God. 'If He's real,' Jack told the butcher, 'He's cruel!'

When he saw Maria planting lavender by the ruined church, he scoffed. 'Waste of time,' he muttered. 'God doesn't live here anymore.'

But something about her stayed with him. The way she moved—slow, deliberate, like she was listening to something no one else could hear. The way she smiled at the magpies, as if they were old friends.

One afternoon, Jack found a sprig of rosemary tucked into his mailbox. No note. Just the herb, fresh and fragrant. He stared at it for a long time before placing it on Ruth's chair.

That night, he dreamed of his wife, Ruth. Not the way she looked in the hospital, but younger—laughing, dancing barefoot in the rain. She whispered something he couldn't quite hear, and when he woke, the house smelled faintly of lavender and woodsmoke.

He went to the church the next day and found Maria sweeping the steps.

'I didn't ask for anything,' he said, voice rough.

'I know,' she replied. 'But Ruth did.'

Jack blinked. 'She's gone.'

Maria looked up, eyes steady. 'Love doesn't vanish. It waits.'

He stood beside her in silence. After a while, she handed him a small stone—smooth, warm, etched with a cross that looked hand-carved.

'She wanted you to have this,' Maria said.

Jack didn't ask how she knew. He just held the stone in his palm, feeling its weight. Its warmth.

That night, he placed it on Ruth's chair, beside the tea. And for the first time in years, he prayed. Not with words. With memory. With the ache that softened into hope.

Maria hadn't planned to stay in Wattleford. She'd come for answers, not revelations. Her grandmother Linda had died years ago, and the stories surrounding her were too strange to trust—tales of healing, visions, and a church that breathed. Maria was a journalist, not a mystic. She believed in facts, not whispers.

But the town unsettled her. The way people spoke of Linda— not with pity, but reverence. The way the church, though crumbling, seemed to hum with something unseen. And the mosaic… it shimmered faintly at dusk, as if remembering.

One evening, while exploring the church, Maria stepped on a loose floorboard near the altar. It creaked, then gave way. Beneath it, wrapped in oilskin and tied with twine, was a journal.

She hesitated before opening it. The pages were yellowed, the handwriting looping and elegant. It told stories about townspeople she'd never met, and some she had. A boy who stopped screaming in his sleep. A woman who found peace in silence. A farmer who saw his wife's face in the clouds and wept for the first time.

But it wasn't just the miracles. It was Linda's voice—gentle, honest, never claiming power. She wrote of doubt, of loneliness, of nights when she questioned everything. And yet, always, she returned to prayer. Not as ritual, but as conversation.

Maria closed the journal and sat in the pew, the light slanting through the broken window. She didn't know what she believed. But something in her shifted—like a door opening, or a breath held too long finally released. She began to visit the church daily. Not to pray, at first, but to read. To listen. To feel.

One morning, she brought her own notebook and wrote about Linda. About the mosaic. About Jack and the rosemary. About the ache in her chest that felt less like grief and more like longing.

She started a blog. The blog post went viral. People wrote from all over—sharing stories of loss, of hope, of quiet miracles. Some came to Wattleford. Others sent letters. One woman mailed a stone etched with a cross, saying, 'I don't know why, but I felt I should.'

Maria placed it on the altar. And when she finally knelt to pray, it wasn't to ask for proof. It was to say, 'Thank You, Lord.'

Maria then posted Linda's journal entries online, one by one, pairing them with reflections from townspeople who had known her—or been changed by her. The stories spread like seeds on the wind. People wrote back. Some shared memories. Others sent donations. A few simply said, 'I don't believe in much, but this moved me.'

One morning, Maria found a note pinned to the church door. It was unsigned, but the handwriting was unmistakably Jack's. He suggested re-building the Church.

By the end of the week, a dozen citizens had gathered at the church steps. They brought tools, timber, and flasks of tea. No one gave speeches. No one asked for titles. They simply began.

The roof came first, patched with corrugated iron and salvaged beams from the old railway station. Then the windows, fitted with glass donated by a retired glazier who'd once sworn off churches entirely. He etched a single word into the corner of each pane: *hope*.

Artists painted a mural of the risen Christ looking down at sunrises, gum trees and hands reaching toward stars. Maria stood back and watched it unfold. It wasn't a revival.

It was a remembering. It was faith. Faith in God and hope for the future.

The building seemed to hold the silence like a blessing, so they named it *The Church of the Listening Christ*. People came to sit, to breathe, to speak aloud to the stillness. Some prayed. Some didn't. All were welcome.

On the day of its reopening, Maria placed Linda's journal on the altar, beside a mosaic tile salvaged from the original floor. The tile shimmered faintly in the morning sun, casting colours across the pews.

Jack lit the first candle.

'I still don't know what I believe,' he said, voice steady. 'But I believe in her. And I believe in this.'

The congregation stood in quiet agreement.

Outside, the wind stirred the eucalyptus leaves. Inside, the light of Christ shone on the congregation.

And somewhere beyond the veil of time, Linda smiled.

Flight to Egypt – and Return

ROBIN PAYNE

'Wake up, Mary!' My husband pulled me up from deep sleep. 'You must get up.'

'Why?' I murmured. 'What's going on?'

'I had another dream. We have to leave! Now!'

Joseph was so insistent that I dressed hastily while he told me what an angel, a messenger of the Lord, had said: *'Get up, take the child and His mother. Flee to Egypt. Remain there until I tell you. Herod will search for the child, to destroy Him.'*

Was this really a message from the Lord? Or Joseph's imagination? His earlier dream was clearly from Him.

Joseph had been in a quandary, learning that I was pregnant (not by him, of course, but by some miraculous work of God's Spirit). After agonising over what to do, the dear man had decided to quietly break off our engagement, so as not to publicly disgrace me.

Then he dreamed an angel of the Lord told him, *'Do not be afraid to take Mary as your wife. The child she conceived is from the Holy Spirit. Mary will bear a son.'* We must give Him the name Jesus, for *'He will save His people from their sins.'*

That was what the Lord told Joseph then. It fulfilled God's promise, through the prophet Isaiah, of a child who'd be called Emmanuel, which means, *'God with us!'*

God with us? This tiny life growing in my womb? God in *me?*

Joseph felt overwhelmed to learn all this. But when he woke up, he did as he'd been told. He quickly organised for us to be married. Joseph trusted what God was doing, even though it was difficult for him. Which made a big difference to me of course, carrying a child. In due course our babe was born, in Bethlehem, where Joseph's family's ancestral home was.

Now Joseph had *another* dream. So of course I took notice and roused myself. Though I was very tired after a strange visit from a group of wise men from the east. Astrologers, they were, serious scholars. Quite wealthy. They told us all about how they'd found us— but that's another story. We invited them into the house where we'd been staying with some of Joseph's family since we arrived in Bethlehem. Their faces lit up when they saw our son, a toddler by now. They knelt down… and worshipped Him! And, you won't believe this, they offered Him gifts of gold, frankincense, and myrrh. Seriously expensive gifts. We didn't know then how much we'd need them.

Everyone knew how ruthless Herod was. If he was intent on destroying our child, he would see to it. So, in the middle of the night, trying not to panic, we woke our child and said sad farewells to relatives who'd woken up too. They gave us some provisions and we left straight away on the long journey towards Egypt. We kept looking over our shoulders, anxious that we might be caught, but tried to keep trusting God in our precarious situation. As refugees we depended on the hospitality of kind strangers to find places to stay overnight.

Just the sixty-five kilometres to the Egyptian border took us a few days. Then we continued for another ten days or so to eventually find refuge among the community of our people there. There were about a thousand Jews in Egypt at that time.

Egypt never felt like home. We hoped to return to our own country when it was safe. Strange coincidence, isn't it? We lived in Egypt just like our people centuries ago. God rescued them from slavery in Egypt through Moses. I remembered Hosea's prophecy, *'Out of Egypt I have called My son.'* That beautiful passage about God's astonishing love for them, as precious children, a love that endured even when they turned away from God. When I felt down, those words helped me to trust God and hold on to hope that God wouldn't abandon us in Egypt. He would bring us out again.

I wondered about the name that Joseph had been told to give our child. Jesus means *Rescuer* or *Saviour*. Would He lead an 'exodus', another rescue? Was my son going to be a new Moses, rescuing our people?

Traders brought news about the disaster after we escaped from Bethlehem. Herod had already been planning to get rid of the child who was born 'king of the Jews' as those men from the east had told him. They thwarted Herod when they didn't return to Jerusalem to reveal exactly where to find our child. Herod flew into a rage—as usual when his power was threatened—and sent a detachment of soldiers to Bethlehem. Their orders? To kill all the little boys two years old and under.

Can you imagine? Burly soldiers knocking on doors, seizing babies and toddlers to slaughter them, right before their parents' eyes. We heard gruelling accounts of the terrible tragedy. About twenty dear little boys out of Bethlehem's population of a thousand were killed in cold blood. Our own vulnerable son was protected, but this came at a terrible cost.

How could God allow that to happen? He wonderfully shielded our dear child from a dire fate. But what about those other parents and little ones I knew well? Why did God not stop this cruel tyrant? Talk was rife that Herod had already executed possible rivals to his throne, including one wife, three sons, some cousins and other relatives. At a bathing party at his pool in Jericho, he playfully ducked a young brother-in-law under water and then held him down until he drowned. And then all those innocent children! I shudder to think of the atrocity. My heart aches for those families.

I struggled to trust God after hearing about the massacre of those defenceless children! But who else could I hold onto but God? I know in my bones He keeps working out His loving purposes, even in the face of the most horrendous evil. Thinking of the appalling trauma Herod caused, I remembered heart-rending words from Jeremiah.

> *'A voice was heard in Ramah,*
> *wailing and loud lamentation,*
> *Rachel weeping for her children;*
> *she refused to be consoled, because they are no more.'*

The heartache experienced in Bethlehem that year was like the terrible outpouring of grief when the Babylonians defeated us some five hundred years before. Babylonian soldiers mercilessly killed men women and children. They forced into exile survivors of siege and famine. It was as though those words of the prophet Jeremiah were being fulfilled once again, in our day.

But you know what? Those heart-wrenching words in the book of Jeremiah are embedded amid hundreds of other words about God's everlasting love. His unfailing compassion and promise of hope for the future beyond the tragedy. Even human tragedy can somehow be understood within the overall loving purposes of God.

I could only pray that the grief of my dear friends back in Bethlehem might be held and embraced in the loving-kindness of our God, who shares our pain. That's what happened for me later. Years afterwards I watched my beloved son taken away from me to the cruellest possible suffering and death. In that horrific grief I was enfolded in the arms of God. I really don't know how people cope who don't feel His loving embrace in their pain and sorrow.

Horrendous things happen in our world. Evil people do atrocious things. But as I learned later, that ghastly death my son faced was not the end. He experienced the absolute worst evil. He took it all upon Himself, and… came through death itself. Alive again, forever. Suffering, tears and pain, death itself will never have the last word. God's loving purposes for good continue and we wait for the day when everything will be set right, when He returns.

That brutal tyrant Herod died in what you call 4BC. That's a fact of history. That's 4 years before your dating system begins. My son was born around the year you call 6 BC or maybe 7 BC. I'm not quite sure how it fits to your dating system. Nor can I remember how long we lived in Egypt but Jesus grew from a toddler into a little boy.

In Egypt, Joseph had *another* dream. This messenger from the Lord said, *'Get up, take the child and His mother, and go to the land of Israel. Those who were seeking the child's life are dead.'* Again, Joseph organised an exit. This time we had longer to prepare and to farewell friends we'd made.

We stayed overnight many times along the way. Near the border, we heard disturbing news. After Herod's death, his kingdom had been divided up among three of his surviving sons and Archelaus had become ruler over Judea and Samaria. Just like his father, Archelaus was ruthless and cruel. We heard that while Herod was on his deathbed, two popular teachers with their followers had removed that terrible sacrilege, the Roman golden eagle, from the entrance to our temple in Jerusalem. They were burned alive! Protests followed. Archelaus had three thousand killed during the celebration of Passover. Such tyrannical brutality continued. Eventually, as we learned later, a deputation went to Rome to appeal to the emperor to have Archelaus deposed. Then a Roman governor was installed—another story…

Worried about Herod Archelaus, we changed our plan to return to Bethlehem. Joseph's fear was confirmed in another dream. So we lengthened our arduous journey by travelling east of the Jordan river, bypassing Judea and Samaria. Finally we crossed over into the area of Galilee. Joseph decided we'd make our home in Nazareth, where my family came from. It was a small and remote farming village of around five hundred people. Other than derogatory taunts that 'nothing good ever came out of Nazareth' it was so obscure that it never got a mention in the history of our people. Unlike Jerusalem or Bethlehem.

Here we'd raise Jesus, safely we hoped, a 'small town boy' from an out-of-the-way place of no significance. After years of exile and dislocation, God had gone before us at every step of the way. He provided for us, kept us safe in his loving care, even through our hardships and griefs. I was learning to trust God's loving goodness—a lesson I needed to keep repeating through the rest of my life.

Safety for our son proved to be elusive. He was eventually betrayed by evil schemes plotted against him. He experienced hatred, cruelty, torture and death—the worst imaginable. There was nothing I could do to save him. Yet I came to understand that death was the way He indeed saved us—from our sin, from the power of death, raising us up with Him to the new life of His resurrection. Words from the prophet Isaiah, fulfilled in my son, encouraged me:

> *… He became their saviour*
> *in all their distress.*
> *It was no messenger or angel*
> *   but His presence that saved them;*
> *in His love and in His pity He redeemed them;*
> *   He lifted them up and carried them all the days of old.*

I hope you know that for yourself too. Thanks for listening to my story.

Hosea 11:1
Jeremiah 31:15
Isaiah 63:7–9
Matthew 2:13–23

Mother's Heart

JEANETTE O'HAGAN

Chavah stirred the pot of bubbling lentils, one hand pushing the wooden stick, the other massaging her aching back. Six months carrying this child and already he made his presence felt. She loved all five of her children, but her first born, Kayin, big and strong from pulling up tree stumps and ploughing stony soil, gave her the most joy. Surely, he was the promised one who would bruise the serpent's head. He would end the struggle their lives had become and restore paradise.

Fragrant steam, heavy with woody scents of mushroom, root vegetables and herbs, bathed her face. She replaced the lid and, using a softened lambskin, shifted the pot to the side of the fire.

Excited chatter came from the house where her daughters made ready for the harvest ceremony. Her two sons, young men now, walked up from the stream, hair wet and faces shining. Avel, taller than Kayin, a dreamy look in his dark eyes, seemed slight beside his older brother, with his flaming red hair and confident stride. Their father, Adamah, his skin sun-dark, walked behind with a slight limp.

The younger two girls, Talitha and Lehevah, burst through the door curtain and ran towards the menfolk, piping questions. The eldest girl, Naomi, hung back, her grey eyes thoughtful.

Life was hard since they'd been exiled from the mountain valley with its verdant fruit trees and thornless bushes. Chavah sighed, guilt searing her heart. Why had she listened to the shining, sweet-talking beast? He'd lied to her and to Adamah, standing silent beside her. The sweet fruit with the bitter aftertaste had stripped them of innocence and broken their communion with Elohim Adonai. No longer could they walk with Him as breezes whispered through the garden. Resentment and blame fractured their own relationship.

Now work that once seemed easy came with sweat, pain and sorrow. Their world's harmony ruined.

'Come!' Adamah called, waving Chavah and the girls over to the sacred stone under the spreading sycamore tree. 'Bring a gift of your very best for Elohim.'

Her family gathered in a semi-circle, each with their chosen offering.

Adamah raised his arms to the deep heavens above. 'Adonai, we thank You for providing new lambs and kids, for ripening fruit and a rich harvest of grains. We pray You keep Your face towards us in grace and mercy. We ask Your blessing in the year to come.'

He signalled to their youngest, Lehevah, *little dove,* to place her offering on the altar. She brought a woven basket of new herbs from her small garden—mint, dill and cumin. Talitha placed a carved pot of new-gathered honey and Naomi some fresh-baked loaves of barley bread. Avel, stepping forward with a shy smile, laid a young lamb on the altar.

Then it was Kayin's turn. He placed a basket laden with grain, plump vegetables and figs beside his siblings' offerings. 'Elohim, accept this fine fruit I've wrest from the hard earth with my own strength.' His face glowed with pleasure at his achievement.

A cloud covered the sun, casting them all in shade. Lightning flashed and sizzled. Thunder reverberated, vibrating through Chavah's heart. The gifts blackened in the leaping flames— all but Kayin's untouched basket. The bright confidence, the easy pride fell from his face, like skin stripped from sinew. He hurled a daggered glance at Avel.

No one moved. Always before, Elohim had accepted *all* their offerings.

Chavah placed a comforting hand on Kayin's shoulder. 'Who knows the ways of Elohim? Come my children, the food is waiting.'

Avel ran his hand along his carved staff. 'Later, amma. I must enclose the flocks before nightfall.'

Lehevah grabbed Avel's arm. 'Avel, won't you eat with us? All day, we've prepared a splendid feast to celebrate the bountiful harvest.'

Avel tousled her dark hair. 'No, little sister. Didn't you hear lions roaring in the hills last night? The sheep and goats need protecting. Save me some of your sweet honey cakes.' He grabbed his cloak and strode off.

Naomi placed a hand on Kayin's arm. 'Brother, come and eat. Amma made your favourite—lentil stew.'

Kayin didn't respond, his gaze fixed on his brother's retreating back.

Adamah took Lehevah's hand. 'Come, child, your brother will join us soon.' He nodded to Kayin and led the girls towards the feast. He flicked a pointed glance over his shoulder to Chavah—the look he sent when anything went wrong.

You fix it; this is all your fault, it said. *If only you hadn't listened to that serpent.* As if he hadn't stood right beside her the whole time. The serpent had beguiled them both.

Chavah reached out to her eldest. 'Kayin, my love, I'm sure this means nothing.'

For surely, he was the promised redeemer who would bring them home to the fertile mountain of Gan Eden or turn these plains into paradise. How could Elohim be angry with her beautiful son?

'Amma, how can you say so? I worked from dawn break to sunset. I spend long hours wrestling stones from the obstinate earth beneath a scorching sun. I pulled out thorns and thistles and carried water to the thirsty fields. I chased marauding animals. I worked harder and longer than abba who can no longer do a full day's work with his injured leg. Harder than Avel who floats like a wayward cloud, drifting here and there with his precious flocks. How can his offering be accepted and mine be rejected? Nobody works as hard or as well as I do.'

Chavah sighed. She loved her eldest but knew his weakness. He saw only his own work as important and disparaged the contributions of others. Jealousy of his younger brother eroded their relationship. This rivalry, if she was honest, wasn't helped by parents chipping at each other and having their favourites.

'Son, eat with your family who love you.'

'I am not hungry.'

She knew that obstinate I-will-not-be-moved look. 'Then seek Elohim and ask Him why he found no pleasure in your offering today. Don't listen to the serpent's voice! I'm ashamed I did.'

'I am not weak and gullible like you or abba. Am I not the son who will strike the serpent's head?' He shook off her hand and stalked away into the fields.

Her throat tightened. Did he really think so little of her? 'Kayin,' she called. 'Don't do anything foolish.'

Chavah twisted the thread on the hand loom, weaving the threads into a new garment for her son. The aftermath of the gloomy feast had long been cleared away. Blue shadows lengthened on the dry ground, yet neither of the boys had returned.

A grinding stone weighed down Chavah's chest. Her breath tightened as time stretched. The feeling that something terrible had happened congealed and solidified with each beat of her mother's heart.

Avel often spent night in the pens with his flocks if he feared a predator prowled, but Kayin never missed the evening meal. A wind blew up scattering leaves across the bare ground. Putting away the weaving, Chavah grabbed her cloak. 'Naomi, watch your sisters. I'm taking a walk.'

Chavah hurried off in the direction Kayin had gone, her heart seizing when she noticed his tracks curving away towards the direction Avel had taken. She picked up her pace. Along the wadi, overturned rocks, crushed vegetation and deep furrows like bloody gashes pointed to a struggle.

She looked around, eyes skittering around the valley, seeing only the scattered flock dotting the shadowed gullies, wandering without a shepherd. She shivered as though suddenly drenched in a torrent of rain. 'Please, Elohim Adonai, no.' She dropped to her knees and bowed her head. 'Where are my sons?'

The burnished light of sunset caught a large flat stone in front of her. Too red. She reached out to touch it, her fingers recoiling from the sticky wetness. *Blood.* An animal's, perhaps. But the strands of dark curly hair stuck to the rock didn't come from a sheep or goat.

No. No. NO.

She had to find her strong, young men. See their merry eyes while they explained that all was good between them, and that she worried over nothing.

She pushed down sobs threatening to convulse her and examined the ground in the fading light. More tracks, these deeper with staggered steps, as if someone carried a heavy burden up the slope. She followed the trail into a gully running like a scar cutting deep into the hillside. There, a dark figure, hunched and broken, crouched in the shadow of a cave. Kayin.

Chavah ran towards her first-born child. Her gaze raked the gully for a sight of her mischievous, light-hearted younger son, looking for his carefree grin, denying the deepest terrors of her mother's heart. But deep down she knew that Kayin's stance carried shame, recognising in it her own and Adamah's attempt to hide their failure when their sweet harmony with Elohim Adonai had ruptured.

'What have you done?'

'Not you too!" Kayin swung around to face her, his voice a deep bear growl.

She staggered backward, speechless. An angry red mark marred his face. It zigzagged down his forehead to the bridge of his nose. His eyes were wells of darkness, his tunic as darkly stained as his hands and his heart.

The broken body of his brother lay sprawled at his feet. Limbs limp, head lolling with a gaping, bloody wound at the temple. Avel's eyes stared sightlessly at the sky.

Bitter bile churned her stomach and scorched her throat. This. This was death. Her younger son, the first of their family to taste its terrible sting.

So sudden, so unnatural, so final.

'Kayin,' the words were torn from her throat. 'What have you done? You were meant to save us, to protect your family, not bring more judgment upon us! Adamah...'

What would her husband do, when he learned Kayin had killed his favoured son? If Elohim had rejected Kayin's offering, what punishment would he give to one who had destroyed an image-bearer?

Agony twisted Kayin's face, then blazing anger. 'Do you think I care? Elohim rejected my offering — for no good reason. Now he has marked me as a warning to any who would harm me in revenge for Avel's killing.' His face convulsed.

'An accident, tell me it was an accident.' Her gaze slipped to Avel's life blood drying dark on his brown skin, matting the curls to his head. She swallowed hard and stretched out a trembling hand. 'Come home with me. We'll talk about it.'

'No. Elohim sends me to a land far to the east as punishment for taking my brother's life. I cannot resist His command.' He looked over her head, refusing to meet her eyes. 'I... I am no better than my parents. I heard the serpent's voice deep in my heart. Elohim warned me, but I refused to listen. Now my brother is dead, and I am cursed to wander far from home and family. Only this mark is Elohim's protection. I'm sorry.'

Kayin flung back his head and roared in deep guttural pain. Grabbing Avel's carved staff, he staggered away into the gathering night.

Chavah sank onto the ground, her heart shattered stone. She had lost both her sons. The curse that had ran like a fault line through their lives since their exile from Gan Eden widened in a heart-rending chasm.

'Wasn't he the one?' she moaned. 'Didn't You promise?'

~Daughter, the One is still yet to come.~

She lay a hand on Avel's shoulder, his smooth skin cold as the ground beneath her. 'My sons are gone.'

~Avel is safe in My loving arms. Kayin still lives, an exile, but protected.~

How could she bear this grief? Would her overreaching pride, her mistakes and those of her husband haunt her children's lives forever? How long must they wait until the promised one brought Elohim Adonai's healing? What would it cost the world?

She wanted to give them love, yet she was never enough. 'All that I touch is failure.'

A wind stirred as the sun slipped below the horizon, cooling her face and stroking her hair with a tender touch.

~My child, lean into My strength and love. I am enough.~

A barrier broke inside her. She let go of pride. Amid her shattered soul, the landslide of guilt and grief, a seed of stillness and peace burrowed deep and bloomed into peace.

She stood, brushing the earth from her tunic and headed down the hill to her family.

The Death of Moses

ANNE HAMILTON

*J*ust a little further, Joshua. Thank you for humouring an old man. You've been patient, uncomplaining—as always. Not like my brother and sister.

Ah, forgive me. I speak ill of the dead. Forget my criticism—remember only their encouragement and support, blessed be their memories.

Not too far now. Up past this outcrop, and over there. There—where I can see the land one last time. Where I can see the promise stretched out before my eyes. The white salt flats, the black of asphalt, the silver of the sea, the gold of the hills, the blue thread of the river. I imagine the sounds and smells—oh, and the tastes too. Remember that enormous grape cluster you and Caleb shouldered all the way back from Eshcol? Did I ever tell you that, long after we'd finished sharing its bounty, its sweetness lingered on my tongue for months?

You are too silent, Joshua. Do not grieve.

I am glad to show you this vista on such a beautiful day. I had only a brief view last time I was here. Dust haze too quickly hid the glory of the land the Lord has pledged to us. But no sandstorm threatens us today.

That is well, for I do not know how much time is left. Only that the summons has come.

You remember all that I told you, Joshua? Where to go? What to watch out for? The Prophet like me the Lord will send? Be of good courage. Be strong as you contend for the inheritance of our people.

I will bless you before I go, before I fall asleep and the kiss of God draws my final breath from me. But listen first to my command: begin each day with the thought that the Lord is with you. He is your salvation.

Ah, I saw a flicker of a smile disturb your sadness. Remember all our conversations about salvation? The first time I called you 'Joshua' and you laughed, thinking I'd got your name wrong? 'Hosea,' you said, correcting me kindly by adding, 'your servant.' And I rebuked you. 'No,' I said, 'you are not named *salvation*. Never forget it. You are Joshua, *the Lord is salvation*. Rely not on yourself, nor on your own understanding but on the path He lights before you.'

Let me sit on this rock. No, don't fuss. I will be careful. I have not done so well of late when it comes to rocks, have

I? I have been tested and found wanting. I should not have dishonoured God by striking that rock. Nor should I have doubled down on the dishonour by asking to enter the land of promise another way—through the white mountains of Lebanon. Learn from my mistakes, Joshua. Do not despise the Lord's grace.

My heart is heavy, so heavy.

I think I will lie down. Do you mind if I recline as I bless you? If I close my eyes? If I doze a moment before collecting my thoughts?

I see a long tunnel and a glow at the end, soft as lamplight. The gleaming beckons. It brightens—as searing as the sun, right through my closed eyelids. I am dream-dazzled, even as I slip the bonds of earth.

I must get up. The brightness wakens me. And ah, yes, I promised you a blessing for your journey before I go. It's hard to see. I can only make out dark figures silhouetted against the light. It's freezing here too.

Wait, this cold stuff is snow. How is that possible, Joshua? Did I doze off longer than I thought?

Oh… oh… *oh…* Joshua, *look!* The white peaks of Lebanon. How did we get here? We were at Nebo, just a moment ago, high above the desert.

Joshua? Is that even you?

Don't nod at me like that.

What's happened to you? I hardly recognise you. Your clothes are shining. They're even whiter than the snow here on the ground. And your face. It's radiant.

Listen, take my advice. When it happened to me, I wasn't aware of it and it greatly alarmed people. You'll need to hide your face until it fades. Keep quiet about it too.

This is all too strange. How did you enter the Presence of the Lord and yet I failed to notice it? I don't understand any of this, Joshua. What is going on? Why am I here?

And who are these three strangers? Friends of yours? How is it that I've never met them, then? Where do they come from? I can hardly make out their accent.

So…

…are they really serious about building us tabernacles?

Based on
Deuteronomy 34:1–8
Matthew 17:1–9

AUTHORS

ANNE HAMILTON

Anne was a mathematics teacher for 30 years before she decided one day it possibly wasn't her calling. She then realised she'd better apply for some jobs to practise her interview skills. The first position she tried for was at *Vision Christian Media* and she was appointed the Australian editor of the devotional, *The Word for Today*. She is a speaker, editor, counsellor and award-winning author of over 50 books. Listen (or read) her podcast at gracedropswithanne.com

DELL SADDLER HAMILTON

1930–2022

Dell was an agent of grace and healing to many wounded people all around the world. She ministered in Australia, New Zealand and Asia and often hosted many people from interstate and overseas who came to seek out her wisdom. She always wanted to write a book on angels and miracles. Included in this collection is one of the short stories she wrote about her true-life experiences before she died.

DIANA DAVISON

Diana Davison lives in Brisbane, Queensland. Her work has appeared in — various poetry and short stories anthologies here in Australia plus online journals and publications overseas. She has been nominated for the Touchstone Awards for Individual Poems 2025 and remains inspired by nature, family and the constant changes life presents. Her memoir, *Tickled Pink!*, is a 2026 release by Armour Books.

HAZEL BARKER

Hazel was born in Burma of an Iranian Muslim father and an English Catholic mother. Blacklisted by the Burmese Junta, she fled to Australia, where her heart's desires were fulfilled when she married the boy of her dreams. Her short stories, memoirs and literary novels have won many awards. Three were finalists in the Australia and New Zealand CALEB Competitions of 2017, 2019 and 2022, respectively.

INGRID DACKER

Born in Sweden, **Ingrid Dacker** has lived most of her life in Australia. Love for God and His family shines through her writing. Ingrid's warmth and insight colour her work with hope and encouragement. She also enjoys creating art, knitting, pottering in her garden and delighting in her grandchildren.

JEANETTE O'HAGAN

Jeanette O'Hagan began spinning tales as a child. Her Nardvan stories span continents, millennia and cultures. Some involve shapeshifters and magic. Others include space stations and cyborgs. An award-winning author, she has published over forty stories and poems, including *Under the Mountain* Series, *Akrad's Legacy* series and *Rise of the Consortium*. Jeanette has practised medicine, studied communication, history, theology and has a Master of Arts (Writing). She loves pondering life's meaning and communicating God's great love.

JENNY GLAZEBROOK

Jenny Glazebrook lives in country Australia with her husband Rob, four children, and many pets—including a sheep who thinks she's a dog and a goose who thinks he's human.

She feels most alive when she's writing, and is the published author of Christian YA fiction, inspirational fiction, women's fiction, and some devotional works. She loves to encourage others to know and love Jesus and walk with Him each day.

JENNY WOOLSEY

Jenny Woolsey, M.Ed. (Hons), is an author, speaker, potter and carer. She was born with a facial difference and lives with low vision. Jenny is an Amazon best-seller and has published eight middle grade/YA books on being different and a personal development book. Her short stories are published in 23 anthologies. Jenny volunteers in the community and mentors at the Queensland Writers Centre.

JO WANMER

Jo Wanmer writes to tell of her God and the wonderful things He has done. Her first book was written to display God's work in her life. You will find it hidden in the fiction story, *Though the Bud be Bruised*. Her recent books, *El Shaddai* and *El Roi*, display God as a lover of our souls. Her hope is that her reader sees God revealed in her words.

JUDY ROGERS

Judy Rogers is a retired primary Special Education teacher. She is also a leadership Trainer volunteering with Girl Guides Queensland. Judy enjoys gardening, painting, travelling and spending time with her children and ten grandchildren. Her most recent publication is *Nothing Happens By Chance*, a collection of biblical short stories.

JUSTIN YEEND

Drawing inspiration from both Renaissance and contemporary mystical Christian writers, **Justin Yeend** began his journey into writing during his theological studies. This poem marks his first exploration of the four-gospel journey through the contemplative lens of the Quadratos method. Justin resides in Brisbane with his wife and two children.

KAREN ROPER

Karen Roper is passionate about seeing people live their lives the way God intended and to fulfil the purpose and plans that God has for them. She has run several life groups and taught teen church and Sunday school. She loves ministering to others one on one. She has authored two non-fiction books and writes a weekly blog at www.livingthelifegodintended.com

LEXIA MACKIN

With a background as a Workplace Trainer in Adult Literacy within TAFE, **Lexia Mackin** has recently written *Help! I'm a Mum*, incorporating discipleship principles in the family, and *The King's Carriage*, a middle grade chapter book. She is currently writing a YA novel.

LINDA BARTON

Linda Barton, like many women, wears many hats: daughter, wife, mother, and employee. Recently, with the support of family and friends, she co-founded a grassroots charity, *Hike to Heal Australia*, to proactively promote suicide prevention and mental health awareness in her local community. Linda's short stories are written to highlight God's grace, offering hope and inspiration to those in need.

LINDA SHIELDS

Linda Shields has held chairs in nursing and rural health in universities in Australia, UK and Ireland. She is a member of the Board of the Australian Institute for Holocaust and Genocide Studies and is editor of the next volume of its publication, *Genocide Perspectives*. Her published work on nurses in the Holocaust is available on request – l.e.shields@uq.edu.au

BISHOP M. LESTER DIGHTON

Bishop M. Lester Dighton was born and raised in Queensland in a Humanistic environment with strong occult influences. While conducting various occult studies himself, he had an encounter with God which completely changed his life. He is now a self-supported Evangelical Preacher, who works individually with small groups and people in need in a variety of ways, and is a Chaplain to those whom he can serve.

MERRIDY GLAZEBROOK

Merridy Glazebrook loves creation and creating. She is currently in Uni, researching how and why native species use wombat burrows, and has always cared for animals and the beauty God has put in creation. When she is not in the bush or sorting through data, she loves adventuring and thinking deeply, loving Jesus and loving others.

MICHELLE HOPE

Michelle Hope is a writer living on the Sunshine Coast who has been writing stories, books and music since she was young. She is grateful for all the blessings that have unfolded since she found her faith.

MIRANDA DE JAGER

Miranda de Jager grew up in South Africa where childhood challenges cultivated her passion to overcome hardship and encourage others. She started working at eighteen, obtained a degree while working full time and pursued an IT career. Miranda and her husband moved to Brisbane in 2010 and became Australian Citizens four years later. Miranda is fond of reading and enjoys anything creative, including sewing, painting and writing poetry.

NOLA LORRAINE

Nola Lorraine loves weaving words of faith, courage and hope. Her inspirational novel *Scattered* was a finalist in the 2021 CALEB Awards. Her devotional book *Comfort Zone* was published in 2025, with *No Standing Zone* to follow in 2026. She and her husband Tim run a freelance writing and editing business, *The Write Flourish*. She'd love to connect with you through her website: **www.nolalorraine.com.au**

PAMELA JULIAN

As a non-fiction writer, **Pamela** finds the joy and struggles of life experience provide a rich resource for writing from a faith-based perspective. She has had a number of devotions, life stories and poems published in various anthologies. Pamela has commenced a Grad Dip in Creative Writing at Tabor College. Her grandchildren keep her busy.

RAELENE PURTILL

Raelene Purtill has been an active member of the Brisbane writing community since 2012. Her short stories have been published in local and Australia-wide anthologies. She loves to connect with other writers through workshops, retreats and seminars, and to encourage new writers on their journey. To this end she facilitates a local writing group in the northern suburbs of Brisbane. Her work in progress is a steam punk dragon fantasy with Christian themes.

REBEKAH ROBINSON

Rebekah Robinson just wants everyone to fall in love with Jesus Christ. Freelancing via Beckon Creative as a graphic designer, she enjoys writing, singing and worship leading, and may have a slight digital scrapbooking addiction. With 40 years of poetry and songwriting under her belt, Rebekah has also written *Someone to Look Up To* on leadership, and with Anne Hamilton, the first five *Core Values* books in the ongoing *DNA of God* series.

ROBIN PAYNE

Rev Dr **Robin Payne** is a retired Anglican priest, among the first women ordained in Melbourne. Growing up in Sydney, she began her working life as a high school language teacher, has lectured in Old Testament at Ridley College Melbourne, served in parish ministry and, before retirement, worked with local colleagues in a theological college in Central Asia. She is currently involved in ministry at St Mark's The Gap.

ROSEANNE HOLLIDAY

Roseanne is a late diagnosed autistic Christian woman, wife, mother and grandmother. Now retired due to increased carer responsibilities, she had a career as an Occupational Therapist and has been an active participant in various Christian churches wherever she has lived in rural, remote and metropolitan settings around Australia. She has had a strong lifelong inner drive of social justice, advocacy for acceptance, inclusion, collaboration and support for people on the fringes.

ROSEMARY NEW

Rosemary New's writings dig deep from faith's 'wilderness season' following her eldest son's suicide in 1999. Searching for healing and restored inspiration, she discovered Christan Writers, achieving three published short works. Memoir and a novel are evolving between regular online devotional teachings.

Rosie encourages women who are losing faith during distress, with God's promises He never abandons us through our hardships! His goodness purifies our heart and life—per Psalm 27:13.

RUTH BONETTI

Stories of real people, past and present, fascinate **Ruth**. Her classical music career led to chronicling Finnish heritage fighters against oppression in her award-winning trilogy *Midnight Sun to Southern Cross*.

Researching Finnish, Estonian and Russian history, Ruth envisages a book series Musicians Who Changed History with the healing power of music. Her published titles inspire confident performance in words *and* music.

Ruth founded Omega Writers in 1991 to support and encourage Christian authors, and co-founded CASQ in 2023.

SONIA COUCHMAN

Sonia brings over 30 years of ministry experience as a former Salvation Army officer working in addiction and recovery, youth work, congregational ministry, journalism and higher education. More recent curriculum and family violence prevention work with the Lutheran and Anglican churches has informed her research interests, interrogating how denominations position their voice in religious curriculums that form faith in young Australians. Since moving into education, she has served as Chaplain at Melbourne Girls' Grammar and now as a Leader of Boarding at Stuartholme School in Brisbane.

TERRY GATFIELD

Born under the sound of Bow Bells in London when the Luftwaffe was decimating its landscape, **Terry Gatfield** came to Brisbane at the dawn of the hippie and Jesus revolution movements. Tamed by one wife and four wonderful children plus their delightful 9 offspring. Now blissfully enjoying life with a new wife. Went to Bible College in UK, ran a handful of small enterprises. Taught at various Unis, collected a handful of degrees including a doctorate related to economics and marketing. Travelled extensively in Asia, learnt Chinese. Published and conferenced about 100 papers. Retired now in a blissful ecological environment to play the flute, the didgeridoo and write the occasional book.

Y.K. WILLEMSE

Y. K. Willemse (known to friends as Yvette) has been writing works for publication since she was sixteen. With her husband Michael and children Holly and Beatrix, she lives in a small Queensland town, teaching singing and piano. Yvette has a passion for literature written from a Christian worldview. Her books include *Jerry's Window, The Fledgling Account,* and *How to Go Viral and Make Friends by Accident.*

www.ingramcontent.com/pod-product-compliance
Lightning Source LLC
Chambersburg PA
CBHW032226050726
47591CB00001B/276